Hide No More

TJ Michaels

Hide No More ©
Copyright 2010-2015 by T.J. Michaels
Second Electronic Printing – 2015
First Paperback Printing - 2015
ISBN (13): 9780990569947
ISBN (10): 0-9905699-4-2
ALL RIGHTS RESERVED.

Prologue

The woman wished she could move her head, wished she could move anything. Eyes closed against the blinding light overhead, she tried to concentrate on the sounds around her. It all seemed so muted. Fighting against the numbing effects of the narcotic floating in her system, the woman gathered the last of her remaining strength and pulled against the restraints. Nothing. Not a single muscle moved more than a millimeter. Great. Semi-paralyzed and muzzy brained. What a fabulous combination.

She knew full well where she was, also knew there was a horde of white-coated doctors and scientists in the observatory above. They always stayed out of arm's reach when one of her kind was being worked on in what they lovingly called the "Black Carpet Room".

Funny. There wasn't a single thing black in here. She'd know, having been a guest within these sterile circular walls often enough.

"Soldier." A single bland, emotionless voice, louder than the others, floated into the space around her. Immediately the din of conversation bombarding her through the speakers quieted.

"State your rank and serial number."

Immediately, she responded with a clear voice. "Senior Commander, SH-58R39C."

Well, at least her mouth still worked, so she could tell them to kiss her perfect, genetically modified ass.

"State your current assignment and generation, Commander," the scientist said, sounding beyond bored. Perhaps he was. After all, she had a feeling she was here for a reason that was all too common these days among her fellow Gen8s.

"I repeat, state your current assignment and generation."

"IMF Special Weapons and Tactics. Generation Eight Super Soldier." Gods, she hated saying that.

For what seemed like the twentieth time, he asked, "Do you understand why you are here in the labs today, Commander?"

Well, she had a good idea, but since she wasn't completely sure, she said, "No sir."

"You are here because your generation of Super Soldiers, you in particular, have not responded adequately to the additional neuro education that is required to…"

At that point, she simply engaged her

auditory implant that allowed her to control her hearing. She turned the filter on and up as high as her brain could push it. The scientist's voice faded to a muted, barely audible, "Blah, blah, blah…" She'd heard enough. If they were going to kill her, just fucking get it over with. Knowing why they were going to terminate her wouldn't change a damn thing.

Eyes closed, with a calm perfected by several journeys through combat hell, she relaxed her breathing and noticed the veins in her eyelids ran mostly east and west. Then she heard a loud schnick. In the next instant, the red of the inside of her eyelids that indicated the lights were turned all the way up, suddenly hit the extreme opposite of the spectrum.

She snapped her eyes open. The whole damn room was pitch black. Even her enhanced vision had trouble making out what was going on around her. The humming of the machines that kept the dose of the narcotics pumping into her body at the perfect incapacitating level all went dead at once. A blur of white coats milled around upstairs. The scientists in the observatory, trained to do everything in silence, seemed out of sorts.

Was that screaming?

Disengaging the auditory filter, her ears filled with the sounds of chaos. What the hell was going on?

The leather bands over her chest and legs were secured with reinforced synth-steel couplings that required a key. That key, a digital chip coded to the locks on the straps, was probably around the neck of the half-zombie-sounding creep who had spoken to her over the sound system before all the lights went out.

Which meant she was screwed. All hell was breaking loose and she was stuck on her back, strapped to a sterile operating table with her ass paralyzed.

"Whatever you do, Scharsi, don't move just now."

Who the hell…? Wait, that voice was familiar, pleasant. Not dead and careless like the other scientists. And there was only one human in the whole facility who called her Scharsi. But it couldn't be. He wouldn't dare…would he?

She started to turn her head to look at the origin of the voice when the straps were literally blown away from her body. It didn't do a damn thing for her nonworking limbs and parts as she tried to heft herself off the table.

"I said, don't move."

"What's going on?" she asked with a croak. Immediately a tube was inserted in her mouth. Water, thank Gods. "How long have they kept me in here?"

"You've been under sedation for four hours. They just brought you out long enough to question you quickly. Rebels have attacked the facility. And…"

"And what?" she demanded.

"And you're scheduled for life termination."

"Life termination? When?"

The figure she couldn't quite make out leaned in close. Facial features were coming into focus now. And his scent, she'd know it anywhere. His warm breath tickled her ear as he said, "Right now."

Tubes slipped from her body. A familiar, but hated, series of needles were removed from her temple, the side of her neck, her chest and the inside of her biceps. Damn that hurt.

The doors to the room slid open, but instead of the typical light from the hallways, it just seemed to get darker. But the tromp of feet she heard entering the room was a sound she would never forget. She couldn't move a muscle. Couldn't fight. Couldn't run. All she could do was accept her fate. And she couldn't blame the doctor near her side who had always been so nice to her. After all, he was only doing his job. Bastard.

This was it. This was the end. The crackle of a body bag, something she was unfortunately familiar with, rustled around her feet, and then encased her totally. The sound of the zipper sent a cold streak of fear snaking its way through the little holes in each bone of her spine.

"Good night, Scharsi," was said with such affection, followed by a prick in her neck just before the last few centimeters of the bag closed out the world.

Good night? Hmm, that was an interesting way to refer to death.

Chapter One

Tanil Taikiji looked out of the window of the sleek shuttle that sped him and his team out toward the less populated suburbs of Ukure. Though there were still a few hours until the day's end, the winter days were short so it was already dark out. Mind fully engaged on the task he'd been sent to oversee, he didn't notice the smudged fingerprints on the window of the rented craft. The men in his unit fidgeted more than usual, strange for seasoned elites such as these. He forced his brow to smooth, though each of them, at one time or another during the short ride from the space port, tapped the mini-comms on their ears. Someone was talking to them behind his back and he had a good idea who.

Tanil gazed unseeing through the pseudo-glass before turning to KE-0V217, a state-of-the-art Gen8 Gamma SS. He was a giant of a specimen with a patch of jet-black, short-cropped hair that looked painted down the center of his skull from front to back. The shaved sides of his big head sported thick black symbols that reminded Tanil of lightning striking against the domes of Aboo Two. His silvery, almost white eyes gave testament to what he was. Amazing how someone with such distinct markings could have a face that reminded him of a bland protein pudding.

"Who has balls enough to contact you, in private, in the middle of a classified mission?"

Smooth as synthsilk and without the least bit of inflection, the SS said, "Last-minute details from Central Command on our next assignment." He didn't break eye contact until Tanil nodded in understanding and turned back toward the window.

Though his gut didn't feel right about it, the explanation made sense. After this assignment, Tanil was scheduled for some rest and relaxation in the Jiborui system. He'd be enjoying the beaches and tropical setting on Jurgia, the third planet in the system, while the rest of these guys headed for their next mission. He couldn't wait for some time off. Tanil wasn't sure if his recent antsy disposition was because of the need for some downtime or fear of what would happen if he didn't drop below the radar soon. If he were going to disappear for a while, Jurgia was the place to do it.

There were a few chilly desert areas on the planet, but Tanil was booked in a more exotic area right on the Krysu Ocean. And given the twenty-four-hour-a-day lifestyle of Jurgia, he could move about at his leisure without worry of anyone wondering what he was doing out at all hours. Maybe he'd even book a ride out to one of the islands off the main continent and do some exploring.

The con in the shuttle beeped. Another incoming message. Tanil ignored it and let the Second-in-Command handle it. It would appear odd if he showed too much interest in the coming mission as he wasn't expected to be privy to the details since this unit wouldn't be under his command. Still, it made him uneasy.

In fact, several times over the last few days of traveling to Ukure, Tanil wondered why he'd been sent to retrieve a nobody scientist so many years after his crime. Okay, so the man had stolen a Gen8 Super Soldier. Bad crime? Sure. Worth Tanil's time? Hardly.

Less than an hour later, grateful he hadn't been sent here for the missing and now assumed dead female SS, Tanil silently signaled his men into position. Two men took the rear of the dwelling, two covered the windows on either side and the two SS would accompany him inside.

Tanil's party approached the front door of Dr. Carl Sabbo's home. Idiot. There'd been enough signs, hints and signals sent the good doctor's way for him to have gotten the hell off this planet by now. What good was having covert contacts in the resistance if you didn't bother to pick up their clues of danger? For a brilliant molecular and biogenetics scientist, the guy obviously wasn't very smart.

And now, Tanil would have to kill him.

One big bang and the door flew open. Two steps into the dwelling, the man on the couch looked up with shock.

"Military Sciences Doctor Carl Sabbo?" Tanil inquired blandly. No answer. No surprise there. He probably wondered how Tanil knew his previous profession. After all, this man had taken great pains to make sure that nobody on this backwater hook-up knew he used to be a doctor for the IMF...in a previous life, of course.

The man seemed frozen in the middle of counting a mountain of plastic cards that no doubt had a lifetime's worth of credits on them.

Tanil repeated, "Doctor Carl Sabbo?"

He plowed on when the man still didn't

answer. "Doctor Sabbo, you are charged with high treason against the Amalgamation, trafficking illegal currency, conspiracy to commit theft and theft causing the termination of Amalgamation property, namely the Super Soldier SH-58R39C."

Finally the frozen man moved very slowly. On his feet, empty hands raised in the air, he spoke.

"The Commander died during the escape from the labs. I'm the only one here. Do you have a warrant?"

"Don't worry, Dr. Sabbo. We're not here for her. Even if she were alive, we're not stupid enough to send this small of a force after her. My name is Captain Tanil Taikiji." Before Tanil could finish his sentence, one of his subordinates spoke from behind him.

"What are your orders, sir?"

Tanil bit the inside of his lip to keep it from instinctively curling upward at the quiet, almost flat line voice that managed to hold an edge of attitude. It came from one of the genetically modified team members. Tanil couldn't remember his serial number right off, but he was sure this soldier was a tenth generation specimen. He hated working with these damn things. Everyone knew Gen10s were fucking sadistic, even for Super Soldiers.

Super Soldiers? Right. Soldiers had honor, morals and a cause—protect the federation and its civilians. However, this particular generation of creatures had none of those traits. Without hesitation, they killed on order, then killed some more without question, care or an ounce of remorse. Nothing like their Gen8 cousins who, though trained to systematically and thoroughly eliminate a threat, still had a measure of honor, though they were often terminated for that honor.

Without turning to address the belligerent soldier, Tanil said, "Take him into custody."

Nobody moved. The fine hairs along the tendon at the base of his skull stretched taut. What the hell was going on?

One of the SS said, "You heard him, boys. Arrest him." The rest of the team entered through the back door and moved in tandem. After several quick whirring pops, a chunk of blood-soaked brains landed on Tanil's cheek, slid down his face and onto the floor. What the fuck?

"I didn't order anyone to fire!" Tanil yelled up into the face of the man his team had decided to obey. "Prepare for termination, asshole. If you can't follow my orders, then what good are you?"

Tanil tapped the mini-communicator over his left ear and said, "Put me through to Central Command."

A blaze of pain streaked across his back, effectively cutting off any words he'd planned to say to his superior about this nutjob he'd been forced to take along on this mission. Another blast radiated just below his shoulder blade. He fell forward and tried to roll away from the source of the agony. Looking up, Tanil came face to face with death. A laser sight landed directly over his heart.

"Sorry, Captain. Just following orders."

* * * * *

Pain slammed into Tanil's chest, back and head. Radiated through what felt like every pore of his skin from his scalp clear down to his waist. It was almost unbearable, but not enough to make him give himself away. If the traitors who'd tried to kill him were anywhere around, he sure as hell wouldn't advertise the fact he still lived.

Sprawled on the floor, his chest barely moved. Though he heard nothing, that didn't mean he was alone. Tanil cracked an eye lid open just enough to take in the scene around him. The scent of blood filled his nostrils. He wondered if it was his or the man who'd been killed in cold blood before his eyes.

And how long had he been out? A quick glance at his wrist said he'd spent an hour unconscious. Shit. He had to get the hell out of here. Tanil didn't believe for a minute that the female Super Soldier was dead, as the IMF claimed. His gut told him that if Dr. Sabbo had survived that fateful day, then so had that SS. And he'd bet old-fashioned Earth money that she was alive, well and living in this house. And Tanil sure as hell didn't want to be around when that particular female got home to find her savior, Dr. Sabbo, killed and his brains and blood splattered across the floor.

His first thought was to contact Central Command to have the bastard that shot him arrested along with the team that hadn't defended him. On second thought, his superiors sent him here and picked the team that accompanied him. There was a strong possibility the treachery he'd uncovered during his private investigation of IMF covert activities had in fact reached the man he'd considered his closest confidant for the past fifteen years. Damn. Trusting anyone at this point was tantamount to shooting himself in the head. Not a palatable thought considering the fire streaking through his chest from his last introduction to a laser rifle.

Fine. He was on his own. Made things a bit tougher. Tough, but not impossible.

First item of business — get moving. What the...? Where the hell was his uniform? His communicator and ID were gone. They'd even taken his damn boots. Rolling to his stomach, Tanil gagged, then swallowed the bile rising up his throat. He simply didn't have the energy to throw up, no matter how wildly his head spun. Easing up on hands and knees, he took stock of his body.

Amazing. Shot twice yet still alive. Tanil's mind flashed back to the last thing he'd seen before blacking out — a laser sight over his heart as he lay on the floor. Even at close range the discharge of the weapon had obviously missed the thankfully still-beating organ. However, the sting of the small oozing hole from the second shot was overwhelmed by the pain of what felt like a fucking crater in his chest where the energy had exited his body from the first one.

Other than a few cuts and scrapes, and the hole in the middle of his body, Tanil was grateful to be pretty much in one piece. The laser fire cauterized some of the wound, so his blood loss was minimal compared to what it would have been if the shooter had chosen a different weapon. But he still bled. Now all he had to do was keep from bleeding out.

Crawling on rubbery legs, he noted the trail of red he left behind, along with the tracks through pieces of flesh and gore that obviously belonged to the late Dr. Sabbo. But where the hell was the body?

Shit. If his team returned, the trail he left through the muck would prove he'd made it out. But then again, they had no reason to come back here—Dr. Sabbo was no longer a threat of whatever he'd been sent here to apprehend him for. The man's body was missing and the place was in shambles. And Tanil was the only one here. It was obvious they expected him to be found and blamed, or at least implicated, and with no identification to prove he was who he claimed to be, he probably wouldn't live long enough to get much farther than the nearest prison hulk. If he wasn't executed on the way, that is.

Sons of bitches Super Soldier backstabbing traitorous motherfu… Sigh. Better save his energy for other things.

Dragging himself into the first bedroom he came to, Tanil almost sighed with relief. A bathroom connected to a bedroom. And that bedroom was scattered with men's clothes. Some ripped and shredded, but plenty of salvageable items all done in the drab Ukurian style. But he wouldn't complain. Instead, Tanil smirked at himself as he took a moment to wash some of the blood and gore from his body as best he could. The first time he'd ever known a SS to botch a kill, thank the Gods.

Sitting on the side of a mussed bed, he salvaged some of the ruined shirts and then bound his wound as tight and thick as he could manage. After pulling on a pair of loose-fitting pants and a jacket, followed by a long coat, Tanil stuffed his bare feet into a pair of loafers. Who in the world wore loafers anymore?

Damn the shoes were tight. Struggling to his feet with a grunt he simply couldn't suppress, he braced himself against the pain and prayed the coat he wore along with the bindings he'd wrapped around his torso would at least stem the flow of blood until he could get himself away from here.

And then what?

He had no fucking idea. But he'd rather bleed out in the street than be found by a SS. Especially a female. They were more bloodthirsty and thorough than their male counterparts.

Thankful for the cover of darkness, Tanil made his way out of the house and into the relatively empty streets. Hunching his shoulders, he stopped a little old man out for an evening walk and learned the trans station to get to the shuttle for the Ukure Space dock stopped two streets down and around a corner. Thank Gods! Now all he had to do was make it.

Gritting his teeth as he forced his feet to move toward his destination, Tanil had an epiphany, a revelation that caused him to stop in his tracks. The pain of the sudden jolt almost took him to his knees. Why hadn't he thought of this before? Agony and near death were good excuses, but not excuse enough.

If he could find the SS, the one Dr. Sabbo had taken years ago, perhaps he could get her to help him. She had to be around here somewhere, considering the man who'd stolen her had lived mere minutes away. And it was in her best interest to hear him out. After all, the very men who'd created her, and now hunted her, had indeed killed her husband in cold blood for an offense that certainly didn't warrant death. Her enemies were now his enemies. But what did she look like? All he knew of her was revealed in a short briefing before he'd come to this forsaken, far-from-everywhere, barely-part-of-the-Amalgamation place. And what he'd learned was recited only as part of the reason they were to secure Dr. Sabbo, trivial detail. Nothing more.

How the hell would he pull off this new improvised plan? He hadn't even seen an image of the female SS. And certainly she wouldn't be walking around with her serial number stamped on her forehead.

He'd even asked his superiors for a vid and had been promptly and none-too-subtly reminded that his target was Dr. Sabbo and not the supposedly dead SS.

Yet just before he'd taken off for Ukure, Tanil's off-the-grid contacts claimed the SS worked at the Ukure Space Port — information he'd wisely kept to himself. Looking down at the bright spots of red just beginning to freckle the shirt under his borrowed coat, relief was too small a word to describe how glad he was, now more than ever, that he'd never given the names or identities of his contacts to anyone.

Determined to make it to the satellite hospital at the trans station, the plan was to run, or shuffle, inside, give a false name to the doctor or Nursotic on duty and get treated. They would record his visit as "medical care given to an unidentified addict". Times like this made him glad that the Ukurians assumed anyone without an ID was unrespectable. And unrespectables were, quite obviously, Rom-heads.

Then he'd board a shuttle up to the Space Port to get passage through the Smith Gate to…to where? Damn it, probably nowhere since he had no credits. The only thing he'd get for free was the ride up to the Port and the medical treatment. Shit, shit, shit.

Don't give up, Tan. You'll think of something. Hell, he'd better. The laser blast may have semi-cauterized his injury, but it still bled and seeped through the skin. The bindings had become slick and now rubbed against the raw wound. It hurt like hell. And the rasp in his lungs gave a clue that he had some internal injuries to see to. Once again, SHIT.

"This is ridiculous," Tanil growled to himself. He'd already waited half an hour and still hadn't been seen by a doctor or even a Nursotic. At this rate, he'd bleed to death before he ever got treatment. Screw it. He had to find a way onto somebody's ship to anywhere. The larger cruisers had medical facilities too. Somebody was going to fucking patch him up somewhere, somehow.

And it had better be soon. The slow loss of blood had begun to take its toll. The leading cause of death to soldiers and civilians alike was trauma. Already he felt the telltale clammy coolness seep into his fingers. His heart rate kicked up and confusion tapped at the edges of his mind. Tanil knew he was a mere few hours from hypovolemic shock. After that, organ failure. Then death.

Wobbling in an unsteady gait to the other side of the trans station, he hauled himself onto the last shuttle headed to the space dock and prayed the pilot would haul ass. Shuffling in his too-tight borrowed loafers, he headed straight to the back of the vehicle, hoping the conductor wouldn't make it this far to check for tickets. The compartment was nicely dimmed for the evening ride and nobody was back there. Except one person.

A woman. A dark skinned, curly

haired…pissed off woman? Her face was calm enough but her body language screamed "fuck with me and your balls are history".

His years in the service kicked in. Something wasn't quite right about this particular female. Tanil thought perhaps he was just weirding out due to blood loss and the pain of the most amazing ache in his back and across his chest. But then again…

What was it about a woman dressed in an oversized trench coat, opened to reveal the ugliest dress he'd ever seen? The thing was four different colors and sagged on her like an old-fashioned grain sack. Strange how thick her neck was, but she didn't appear to be overweight. No, that was muscle, no matter how much she tried to cover it up. But why cover it up at all? Perhaps they didn't like big women on this planet, Tanil had no idea. Regardless of what her clothes looked like, she was absolutely gorgeous. Not because she was some glorious beauty, but something about the way her cheekbones sat, the way her brows arched perfectly.

And all that cacao skin and naturally curly hair in a color so at odds with her skin it was intriguing. That hair was a unique shade of near-blonde, thick and coarse, pulled into two fat braids with a part down the middle. A few strands had come loose near her ear points and wisped against her shoulder.

A pair of manicured brows in the same honey blonde sat above eyes a soft, though strange looking brown. Almost too light, yet dull, as if they couldn't decide whether to be lively or drab. He couldn't quite put his finger on it.

And since he couldn't think of what to say, let alone his next move once he got to the Space Port, Tanil sat across from her and tried to smile. It didn't work. He could feel his lips pull tight against his teeth on a hiss when the shuttle hit a pocket of turbulence as it streaked toward the upper atmosphere.

Gritting his teeth, trying desperately to hold back tears now, Tanil looked down at the floor and stared at the top of the woman's boots? Military issue, top-of-the-line combat-ready boots?

And moving toward those boots was a small puddle of blood. His blood. Damn it. The stuff was dripping down his back, through his coat and down the back of his seat to the floor.

Tanil lifted his head, hoping she hadn't noticed his very lifeforce inching toward her feet. His gaze snapped up. Her eyes blazed with anger. But why? He hadn't done anything to her. Suddenly her nostrils flared, as if she could smell the blood.

The woman looked like a caged randwulf, ready to pounce. Then she moved so fast Tanil wasn't sure he passed out from the pain of his wound, from the expertly formed fist flying toward his face or a combination of the two.

But whatever had finally forced him into the blackness of unconsciousness, he was glad for it. For now.

* * * * *

"Is it done?"

"Yes sir. Captain Tanil has been terminated sir."

"And the data?"

"It was not recovered, sir. Tanil did not have it on his person or aboard his ship. However, the secondary mission was accomplished. The deserter, Dr. Carl Sabbo, has been terminated. He was alone in the dwelling. Female attire was found in one of the rooms."

"Was it hers?"

"Doubtful. The clothing was for a much larger female than the SS specimen Dr. Sabbo stole from the labs. The reports that the soldier died in the escape seven years ago may be accurate after all. That SS was known to be meticulous in appearance and surroundings. The room where the female clothes were found was nothing short of chaos, and not of our making. She doesn't appear to have been here.""

The man on the other end of the communication winced at the clipped, non-feeling tone in the voice that relayed the information. The soldier reporting the task he'd carried out was beyond calm. It was damn disconcerting. Then the man remembered just what he was dealing with, not bothering to complete the thought of whether the soldier was man or machine. It was a state of the art Gen10 SS. Methodical. Ruthless. Unemotional. Almost fanatical in his need to complete an assignment with as much bloodshed and madness as possible. Just as he'd been bred and trained to do.

"Very well, RE-5512SE. Just arrange for Sabbo's body, or what's left of it, to be found by the right people."

"Yes sir. Over and out."

"One moment, soldier. Who fired the shot?"

"KE-0V217, sir."

"Thank you. That is all." Vulf disconnected

the call and practically skipped to the door of his office.

Finally the thorn in his side had been nipped. Too bad Dr. Sabbo had to be the excuse to get Tanil to the farthest reaches of the empire just so the Captain, or former Captain, could be quietly put down. Tanil would be missed. After all, he'd been one of the best tactical specialists the Interplanetary Military Forces had ever produced. Now he was nothing. Killed clean and quick.

Vulf made a mental note to send a condolences vid to Tanil's parents.

After all, every plan required the perfect touch.

Chapter Two

Scharsi stood on the bridge of the Futsuka-shi and awaited clearance to leave the Ukure Space Port. Thankful that it was little-used, obsolete and out of the way, she wasn't the least bit worried that anyone would recognize the ship, even though it was the same vessel Carl had kidnapped her with so many years ago. The thing had been stored ages ago in a private hanger on the space dock for just such an emergency. She'd had all identifying marks stripped off and replaced with counterfeit ID chips, name and ownership information.

At least the pirates who sneaked over from Free Space were good for something, including keeping her ship in good working order. It had taken no time to get fully stocked, powered up and ready to launch. The space traffic controller's tower floated in the blackness of space, visible from her spot on the docks. Scharsi wondered for the millionth time in just a few short hours what the hell could possibly take so long to get waved through the launch queue.

"Computer, how many ships ahead of us?"

She knew the answer, but felt itchy, almost antsy to get moving. It had nothing to do with the mayhem she'd discovered at her house earlier and everything to do with the unexpected passenger strapped inside a med-tech unit in her sickbay. She'd been in plenty of firefights, bloodbaths, brawls, you name it. Calm had been her forte in the IMF, yet it skittered out of reach. In its place was this uneasy premonition of which she hadn't a clue, yet it was there slithering back and forth across the back of her mind practically hissing at her.

Now at number four in the queue out of the space station, Scharsi kept a vigil watch for any sign of IMF troops, fully prepared to take down anyone who tried to keep her from getting the hell off Ukure. Fingers clenched and relaxed as her thoughts turned once again to the man in the medical quarters. Boundless rage and helplessness assailed her just as they had when he'd first come upon her in the shuttle that carried them from the trans station up to space dock.

Scharsi had had to take a second look. Her first thought was that he was uncommonly handsome. The second thought—strength and stamina—purred through her mind as she took in the wide set of his shoulders and his stocky build, though most of it was hidden underneath a long trench-style coat. Unbidden, curiosity about what was under that coat had taken hold. He had nice hands, long strong-looking fingers. Did he have nice legs with big thighs that could run and run and run? A firm ass rounded by mounds of muscle? And perhaps a cock that…?

Shocked at her train of thought, she'd forced herself to look a little closer. His skin was a strange light bronze, like a man who'd been born with natural golden good looks, then had the blood drained out of him. His brow had drawn tight, then smoothed, only to pull into yet another frown, as if the energy required to keep a calm relaxed expression was something he simply didn't have. He might have had the look of a warrior and a sex appeal that caught the attention of a piece of her she'd thought long dead, but something was wrong with this man.

Then she'd caught a scent so disconcerting that her mind didn't know what to do with it. After a few moments, her affinity for analytics and reasoning kicked in and she didn't like what her senses revealed — blood, burned flesh and…Carl.

The man had moved close enough to drop

into the seat across from her. Only it wasn't his scent that filled her lungs. It was Carl's. Godsdammit. It was one of very few times she'd thanked the Military Sciences Lab for creating her enhanced sense of smell.

The stranger, who now rested in her med-tech, had been dressed like her now-dead best friend from head to toe. He'd smelled like Carl because he'd been wearing Carl's clothes. Which meant he was somehow involved in the carnage she'd discovered splattered all over her living room when she'd gone home early from work just hours before.

Scharsi wasn't sure what made her knock him out in the shuttle. She only knew that for a few moments all reason slipped away from her and she didn't give a shit how he had come to be in Carl's clothes. All she knew was an instant, gut-burning rage that required her to do something. Anything. Obviously an enemy, killing him was first and foremost in her mind, then common sense pushed forward as expected and she'd decided to get answers instead.

"Computer, call me through the con. I will be in the medical bay. I want to know the second we're cleared out of the docks."

"Yes, Commander." She forced herself not to

cringe. Damn it. It was the only thing she'd been unable to erase from the ship's AI memory banks—her rank. Sigh. Former rank.

With that and a quick check of the time, Scharsi deserted the bridge and headed to sickbay. With each step came an unwelcome mix of anticipation and apprehension fused with anger and guilt. Gods, what a fucking mess.

* * * * *

Scharsi stared down at the man she'd cold-cocked in the face. The deep purple bruise over his right cheek bone stood out in contrast to the smooth tone of his skin. An unexpected tide of remorse flowed through her soul at having marred such perfection. Besides, she didn't really know if he was a bad guy or not. He may not have even deserved to be knocked out cold by a woman with her strength—a strength she hadn't bothered to temper or hold back until she pulled the punch at the last second. It was a surprise she hadn't broken his jawbone.

No wonder the IMF thought she'd been unfit to remain Commander of her special weapons and tactics team—she was a damn softy. It didn't matter that she'd been built like no ordinary woman—more like a tank, designed to last and programmed to take out anything in her way. Neither did it make any difference that Scharsi had been bred to kill. Although she was especially good at it, she was still a woman through and through. Physically, the solid mass of muscles gave way to curves at her hips, butt and breasts. But emotionally, psychologically, though conceived in a tube and raised as nothing more than a number with a face and no soul, she had quietly braced herself against the bombardment of the IMF's conditioning. Soaked up all that was of benefit and left the bullshit on the table.

Over the last thirty years, Scharsi had done what very few of her generation of Super Soldiers managed to stay sane and alive long enough to achieve—she'd learned to love herself.

She shook her head at herself and snorted at the memory of the starkness of her life where matters of the heart were concerned. Love was against the rules. Individuality was a crime. Her superiors tried to breed it out of her. Sublim it out of her. Reeducate it out of her. Hell, even beat it out of her. Why? Because unlike many of her fellow SS, not to mention most humans, Scharsi didn't think of herself as a monster or a freak. She wasn't repulsed by what she was, not

34

even when grown men took one look at her and cried as she executed her sometimes morbid duties.

Was she dangerous? Hell yes. Ruthless? When the occasion called for it. But bloodthirsty and vindictive? Not so much.

And when she should have snatched her patient out of the med-tech and held him off the floor by his neck to force his confession, Scharsi found herself fascinated by him instead.

Exactly the reason IMF wanted to "disappear" your ass, Scharsi. Sigh. Now get some information, woman.

Yanking her gaze away from the perfect twin mountains on top of the man's chest—most people called them pectoral muscles—Scharsi entered the command into the med-tech console to administer a sedative, then instructed the machine to begin the repairing sequence. Hopefully she wasn't too late. He'd been unconscious entirely too long and lost a lot of blood. But his stolen clothes, Carl's stolen clothes, had hidden a physique that rivaled her own, yet this man was no Gen8, or any other Super Soldier. There was a story here. While her anger simmered just beneath the surface, tempting her to use any means necessary to get it, an intuition as old as time stayed her hand.

The slightest shuffle of skin against synthsilk caught her attention. She looked down and froze. The man in her med-tech stared up at her with an acute blend of confusion and pain, then of wonder, as if he knew her or something. Damn disconcerting considering she'd never seen him before in her life.

"Talk," she snapped. Other than a shallow steadying breath, her unexpected guest didn't hesitate.

"I have information that could bring the Amalgamation to its knees, or at least aid the factions of rebels fighting against them. Maybe even draw some of your fellow Super Soldiers who've been looking for a way out."

"And who said I was SS," she hissed with narrowed eyes.

"The solid fist that happened to be the last thing I saw before I woke up here told me as much." He tried to chuckle, but spit up blood instead. Poor fella. He looked plain worn out and sounded worse. The way he sucked wind between every three or four words said he was in acute agony. But Scharsi needed more information before she could relieve some of that pain. Interrogation 101 — if the captive is in pain, use it to extract details of their actions. Continue until captive reaches his pain tolerance or breaking threshold. Then, if within your means, relieve said pain long enough for the captive to heal somewhat, then start all over again.

Yep. She knew exactly how to do her job all right.

The man gasped, hacked and then lay still a moment to catch his breath. Finally he spoke again.

"Besides, you fit the description of the female SS stolen by the man whose clothes I borrowed to escape my own death."

"Escape your own death? And I should believe you why?" Scharsi quietly demanded.

"Because I can help you. Even if you hadn't saved my life I'd want to help you."

"Could have fooled me. Last time I checked, you worked for the Amalgamation." It was based on total circumstantial evidence, a total guess, but one spoken to see if he would bite. All the while, Scharsi knew in her gut that it wasn't quite true, but she hoped to make him sweat a little, give her more details. She had to know more.

"I did work for them. It's easier to learn what's going on in the mind of a beast from inside its head."

"Why did your men kill Carl?" When he didn't immediately answer, she snapped, "I'm far from stupid, sir. You may not have been wearing the uniform, but I found your ID in my house."

"That could be anyone's ID, or a plant, a fake…"

"Sure, it could have been, but the GPS chip I disabled and removed from underneath your skin was coded to a military frequency." No need to mention that the wound in various colors of reddish-pink torn tissue and blackened burned skin that went from his chest clear through to his back could only have been made by military issue or bootlegged laser rifles.

"Tagged? I was tagged?"

The man's color rose at an alarming rate. If he didn't calm soon, he'd look like a unripe tomozava. Obviously he hadn't known about the tag. Interesting.

"Sons of bitches," he wheezed. "How the hell did you know to look for it?"

It was obvious he'd been shot by one of his own, or possibly a rogue. Friendly fire, perhaps? But if so, why was he here instead of being looked after by his unit? Each question seemed to lead to more and more questions.

As for Carl's garments, she'd promptly incinerated them the second she'd gotten this guy on board, stripped and into the med-tech.

Scharsi shook her head at the strange turn of events. Her morning started out as it always had, with her going to work and Carl doing his "business". And it had ended with her long-time friend dead and her abduction of an Amalgamation officer. It had been amazingly easy to pull off too. Obviously the idiots providing security for the space port were so self-assured they'd grown ridiculously lax in following their own protocol. All she'd done was toss some Trescalane Tropicure on her guest, then hustled him off the shuttle. When anyone asked, she simply claimed he was drunk. One whiff of his liquor-soaked clothing and they'd waved them on through with nothing more than an annoyed look. No one had stopped her from dragging him into her hanger and aboard her ship at all, though IMF forces were coming in and out of the space dock in numbers.

She turned to the med-tech console and checked his blood pressure and body temp. Didn't look too good. She'd have to let him rest soon. Good thing Carl had stocked this thing with meds. At least something good had come out of his continuing to practice his profession, though it had been nowhere near legal to do so.

"Name, rank and ID," Scharsi demanded quietly while coding the machine to deliver a specific amount of a strong pain reliever.

"Taikiji, Tanil. Captain. IMF security sector nine, ID 4681562. Listen, sh…aaahh, shit that hurts…" His words slurred and fell off. His face twisted into a grimace.

The man was strapped down, yet Scharsi tensed, easing her hand toward the weapon strapped to her thigh. What had he been about to say that began with "sh"? Did he know her code name? No one of the brass did. Only her fellow soldiers and Carl knew her forbidden nickname. Nicknames meant individuality, not something that could be afforded to a walking, talking tool created for a sole purpose — mayhem.

Pain, swift and merciless, assailed her soul at the reminder of her comrades. They'd been bred together, educated and trained together. And some had died together. Yet she'd seen none of them these past seven years. How many were left of her generation?

The thought passed as quickly as it had

appeared as she pushed it away with force and almost snarled at herself. She hated that the old teaching was still there, deep in her subconscious.

Memory surfaced of words snarled into her face as she was forced to push through yet another set of straight arm deadlifts or forced to run yet another kilometer. Or analyze yet another piece of intelligence though her eyes swam from exhaustion. "Love no one. Attach yourself to no one. Invest your emotions in no one. Not even those who save your life. Why? Because your life belongs to the IMF. Remember, if you live another day it will be because it's been granted. By us."

Her benevolent handlers. Fucking bastards.

Shaking herself out of her anger and unexpected self-loathing, Scharsi forced herself to hone in on Tanil Taikiji's words.

"I swear, we can help each other," he said on an unsteady breath.

"Remind me why I should believe you."

"Because the man responsible for your Carl Sabbo's kill order is also responsible for yours and mine. Not to mention the secrets I've managed to obtain during my service. You want to bring them down. I know you do."

But he would become a target if word of his non-death got out. How the hell could he help her if the same people who tried to kill him the first time decided to go for a second shot?

And the most alarming thing of all made no sense-the IMF never left evidence of a kill behind. So why had she found her house full of blood and chunks of charred flesh? And what about the ID carelessly kicked underneath the rug? IMF kills were quick and clean. After all, they didn't want the masses to get wind of what murderous bastards they really were. Perhaps they wanted to set her up for Carl's murder? No, from what she'd heard through the grapevine, she was supposed to be as dead as her unexpected company here. So that left one alternative target — Tanil. And her good ole common sense said they'd been after him.

He was panting now, though still trying to convince her of what she already knew. She should have no sympathy for him or any other Amalgamation asshole. Let him suffer. Just like Carl had. But she couldn't bring herself to do it.

"L-Let me help you bring them down." His gasping and wheezing escalated in direct proportion to how fast the sensors she'd attached to his body fired, indicating his level of stress. "We can help each other. We both have a randwulf in this hunt. You, to avenge your friend. And me, to avenge myself."

His eyes widened as her index finger stretched toward a blue button on the med-tech console.

"Wait!" Tanil yelped. "Think about what they put you through. They made it necessary for Carl to steal you. And to die for you. Just give it some thought."

She turned hard eyes on him, knowing her expression screamed bloody murder.

"I already have, Amalgamation punk."

Scharsi pushed the damn blue button and in seconds Tanil's world fell away as the clear flexi-dome of the med-tech lowered to cover him completely as he sank into oblivion.

Gods, how she wished she could join him.

Chapter Three

Back on the bridge, Scharsi put on a pair of over-ear headphones coded to the Space Port frequency she'd hijacked.

Speaking clearly, but quietly, she said, "Computer, give me a status on the uplink to surveillance system CSAB0942."

"Uplink complete, Commander. Feed will begin in ten seconds."

Scharsi braced herself as the high pitched hum and click in the earpiece told her the hack into the networked security system Carl had insisted on installing in their home was complete. A list of files displayed across one of the bridge control consoles. She selected one with the timestamp closest to when Carl must have been murdered.

"File loaded. Playback will begin in exactly six seconds, Commander."

Every muscle in her body went taut as the audio streamed. Carl hadn't allowed video in case someone else managed to do the same thing she was doing now, and she was glad for it. Why? Because what came through the earpiece would have driven her to recklessness. It was bad enough to hear it all. At the sound of the whir of a laser rifle, her mind conjured the image of it being aimed at Carl. The angry, then shocked cry of her best friend. The quiet squish—a sound she was familiar with—as Carl's body fell to the floor with a quiet thud-flop as he landed in blobs of his own flesh. Then Tanil's mouth opened on a yell that had become a garbled scream even as he tried to get the unit to stop firing.

Moments later she heard the group move around the room, then through the house with the exception of the man who'd shot Tanil. He'd taken a stance near the rear door...just beneath the only video bit in the house that was embedded in the halo-lamp above that door. She got a completely clear image of his face, every line, every wrinkle. Every nuance. Then she saw it—a tell that gave away just who this asshole was. His eyes, a pair so like her own there was no mistaking him as anything but a Super Soldier even if he hadn't been a third of a meter taller than his comrades and just as wide. She'd assumed this was a gang of mercenaries, considering their uniforms were unmarked, but she'd been wrong. This was IMF.

Scharsi rolled it back and watched the communication again from the second the man took position to the end of the whole fucking nightmare. The one making the link said words that caused her jaw to drop. He believed her dead, and that whatever Tanil was supposed to have had wasn't found anywhere in the house or on his ship. Then it was over.

That scant sixty seconds was all she needed to learn that the soldiers who'd trashed her house and killed her friend had been after Tanil all along. She and Carl were just expendable targets. Fucking sons of bitches.

She turned away from the vid, then changed her mind. Eyes back on the console, Scharsi's body went still. The SS creep that'd reported her dead was looking right at her, staring into the hidden surveillance cam as if he knew it was there. But surprisingly, he said nothing to his team. Instead, when one of them approached to report the coast was clear, he'd turned away as if he'd never noticed a cam pointed right at him. Correction, pointed at them.

Even after turning off the vid and walking through the incident in her head, the whole thing remained amazing and highly illogical. Why would the military brass send an entire ops

team way out to Ukure to kill one captain? One
human captain, at that? It didn't make sense but
it did reveal how desperate the Amalgamation
had become in its efforts to stamp out the
slightest hint of rebellion among the ranks.
Either that or they'd gotten wind of what Tanil
knew and was willing to go to any lengths to get
rid of him.

Intuition said it was the latter.

So, Tanil had been telling the truth. He
wasn't responsible for Carl's murder. So who
was? The answer — the superior of the Super
Soldier team leader she'd seen on the vid, the
one who had called to report the deed done.

And that thought led to another. Why the
hell hadn't the SS told his team they'd been
recorded? Anyone who hacked into the feed
could hear what they'd done in the area not
under vid surveillance, then see who'd done the
deed the second they moved toward the exit.
Why did he let her get a good look at his face as
well as every soldier who had left through that
back door? She could identify all of them
now...and the SS had known that.

What the hell was going on?

Some hours later, Scharsi stood still as Earth
stone and watched the human male slowly come

awake again. He'd been out for almost two days now, plenty of time for the med-tech to repair most of his damaged muscle and tissue. He'd be good as new in no time...so she'd better hurry up and decide what the hell to do with him.

"May I have some water, please?"

Without a word, Scharsi enabled the automatic feed. Cool water flowed through the tube taped to the side of his mouth. The control mechanism was attached to the back of his hand. He automatically flexed his wrist. The water flowed in. When he was sated, he relaxed and the water flow ceased.

"Are you a doctor like Dr. Sabbo?"

"No."

"You're good at working this machine, though?"

"Yes."

"Are you going to say anything else besides yes and no?"

"Perhaps." Then she changed her mind. She needed this man to cooperate, which meant she'd need to appear to bend a little. This was a military officer who certainly didn't seem to be the wussy type, though whether he was honorable remained to be seen. And just because she could kill him in a blink didn't change the fact that he was a male. And all males needed to feel at least a little bit in charge, even if they weren't even close. A little wisdom would make getting what she needed that much easier.

So keeping her tone conversational, yet bland, she said, "Carl had this med-tech put in two years ago. He was adamant that I learn to use it. Just in case."

Tanil stretched as much as he was able in the close space of the machine he lay in. But even that little bit of movement made noticeable ripples in the toned landscape of his chest and stomach. Interesting. Even after a couple of days in med-induced heaven, he looked healthy rather than peaky.

She looked closer. No stubble on his face. Her fingers itched to run a path over his jaw just to make sure it was as smooth as it appeared. Then perhaps they'd journey up to his head to ruffle the short crop of dark silk covering it, before trailing down his throat and off to the bulge of muscle at his neck and shoulder joints. All that golden skin sent her mind wandering down a path that it had no business going. Time to change the subject…at least in her head.

"Your pain tolerance appears to be quite high," Scharsi said with no inflection. She was impressed with such a specimen. But he'd never know it. "Do you need more meds?"

"No, thank you. I can't think if I'm pumped up on narcs." His wrist flexed to release another trickle of cool water. After a few swallows and a refreshed sigh, he turned his whiskey brown eyes on her.

"What do they call you?" he asked.

Suppressing the urge to roll her eyes, she answered with perfected dullness. "You already know I am Gen8. Serial number SH-58R39C." It almost killed her to say it after living so many years as Scharsi. As a person.

"No, that's not what I meant. What did he call you? The real you."

An acute grip in the area of her heart threatened to burst through her chest. It was unlike anything she'd ever experienced outside of combat. A glance at the genuine concern in Tanil's eyes filled her with an unexplainable softness. She almost batted her lashes. What the hell? This urge to flirt was new. And the timing was completely fucked up.

She wrenched her gaze away from the temptation lying before her. "He, Carl, called me...Scharsi."

"Mmm. Beautiful name. Almost as beautiful

as you are."

The man was full of shit. Carl thought she was beautiful. This man saw her as a tool. Didn't he?

A verbal alert issued throughout the ship in a disembodied voice. It sounded neither male or female, yet still managed to seem annoyed.

"Clear of Chassir Asteroid Belt. Now approaching Trevosian Joss Dome."

But she didn't want to stop there. The sooner they got to where they were going, the better. Scharsi punched the interlink button on the small wall unit that allowed her to interact with the bridge console of her ship without actually being on it.

"Continue course without refuel at Joss Dome." Several quick taps on the entry keys followed. "Acknowledge receipt of new coordinates and recalculate arrival at final destination."

"New coordinates received. Estimated arrival time to final destination recalculated to approximately five and one half days."

"Request addition to queue upon arrival at Trevosian Smith Gate. Hail destination control thirty-six hours before arrival."

"Yes, Commander," the disembodied voice

replied.

"So, Commander," Tanil hissed. The deep intake of breath hailed the return of major pain. "Where are we going?"

She didn't answer immediately, just watched him with an unblinking stare she'd perfected years ago. He shifted. Merely a rippling of muscle, of barely leashed primal energy. It was the most sensual thing she'd ever seen on a fully human male. Something forbidden, always controlled, reared its head inside of her. Desire—unexpected and untimely. Smashing it ruthlessly into the soles of her boots, Scharsi snatched her focus away from Tanil's body and strode for the door.

She could practically feel the eyes of her "guest" boring through her back. It didn't make her nervous, but it did make her twitchy. Anxious. Yet not in a negative way. It was damn disconcerting.

"Commander, you are being hailed," the con announced.

"Wait," Tanil called. "Where are we?"

She cut across him with more steel in her voice than intended. "The one place neither of us are expected to surface. Now quiet."

She turned and punched the controls on the

wall. Damn.

"Computer, patch directly into this room on a secure channel."

"At once, Commander."

"Hailing designated vessel. This is The Web. Confirm."

Holy shit, what a sexy voice. Strangely enough, the idea of sex made her think of Tanil instead of whoever was attached to the sound currently caressing her through the con. She pushed the thoughts away-she sure seemed to be doing that a lot lately — and focused on this communication. It could mean life-or-death.

"This is S24 confirming," Scharsi replied, deliberately using the ID secretly given to her by the man she'd contacted at The Web the very day Carl had been killed. She deliberately did not mention the name of her vessel. It simply wasn't necessary.

"Do you expect to make the appointed time?" the sexy voice asked.

"Yes sir."

"Enter code and submit through the designated encrypted channel."

She keyed in the password and awaited further instruction.

"Hold," he said. A few seconds of complete

silence ensued. Neither she nor her patient moved a hair. Barely breathed.

"S24, confirmed. Pre-cleared to land on dock four, bay seven at exactly 0430 hours in six days. An escort will be waiting. I'm Sealy. We look forward to your arrival. Out."

"S24, out." A quiet click disconnected the con.

"Do I get to know where we're going now? Or whether I'll remain alive to enjoy wherever it is?" Tanil groaned. "Or if I'll continue to enjoy your company once we get there?"

"Are you flirting with me, Officer Tanil?"

"Please call me Tan, or just plain old Tanil. And yes, I am definitely flirting with you. It's in poor taste, I know, but I can't help it. Maybe it's whatever drugs you gave me," he laughed. Or tried to. It came out more of a strangled chuckle. "Ow. Still a bit sore, but definitely better." He sighed and then said, "Then again, maybe it isn't the drugs. Maybe it's the fact that I almost died. Coming close to leaving this body of mine kind of puts a new perspective on things that I didn't think were important before."

And a sexy-as-hell smirk appeared on his golden cheeks. Now that his eyes were completely open, she could see the tawny brown irises were ringed with gold. They were unique with an almond, almost feline, shape to them. In spite of his obvious discomfort, they sparkled with a hint of mischief. In a word, gorgeous. Just like the rest of him.

Scharsi snorted, then bit her lip to suppress an unexpected chuckle of her own. Not good. She wasn't supposed to be attracted to this man. Or any other man. It would never feel right now that Carl was gone. How could she even think about intimacy with the opposite sex so soon after the one man who'd given everything for her had had his life snuffed out at the whim of some bureaucrat across the galaxy who thought it was his job to determine who breathed and who didn't?

Guilt stripped the almost-grin from her lips and set her feet on a course up to the bridge and away from the sex personified male lying in her med-tech. Decision made, she would trust him to help her bring a killer to justice.

* * * * *

"What the hell is going on?" Scharsi asked herself out loud. She stalked around her ship in a funk, but she couldn't hold the facade for long. Ever honest with herself, it still took an incredible amount of effort to admit, though only in her head, that she was attracted to Tanil on a ridiculous level. If the dancing in her gut, the excitement and anticipation compared to anything, it would be the first time she'd successfully hunted four of her IMF trainers, alone and without detection.

On one of many such tests, they'd flown her and three others out to the desert. The mission- capture the targets without injury to them or yourself while under live fire. Weapons allowed. None.

Her classmates had been taken out into the dunes one by one. Each had returned severely injured. One had died from those injuries.

Her lip raised in contempt at the memory of the pride and jubilation she'd felt at having captured each man all by herself. And as reward for that particular training mission, her handlers had given her her first sweets, and she'd been hooked on lillee candy ever since. She'd been sixteen years old at the time.

Now here she stood, a grown woman trying to keep the lid on her giddiness as she paced the bridge of her own ship like a caged animal. And there was nowhere to run. Tanil's scent was everywhere and the more she caught it, the more her muscles clenched and burned with the restraint she exercised over them. In his presence, she resisted reaching out to touch him. Sinking her hands into the dark hair on his head. Touching her lips to his while running her fingers over his smooth jaw. Gliding over all that golden skin. Gods, the man even had pretty feet. Damn it!

A rustle in the distance grabbed her attention and she groaned. It was him, Tanil, pulling on the clothing she'd ordered up for him before running back to the bridge a little while ago. He'd been sitting up when she strode into sickbay, but he'd appeared a bit shaky, not quite stable at all. A moment of worry crept in that he'd actually fall out of the med-tech.

There went the sound of clothing rubbing against skin. Scharsi turned her auditory filter all the way up. She didn't need to stand here like a hard-up…well, hell, she obviously was hard up. Never mind, cancel that thought.

But she couldn't stay locked up on the bridge forever, hiding from Tanil. She'd never hidden from anyone for any reason other than staying alive. Even on Ukure she hadn't kept a totally low profile. It just wasn't in her nature to be a coward. Yet here she stood, behind a secured door because of one man. Why? Because she wanted him. Wanted him so badly she practically shook with it. He'd flirted with her, but that didn't mean he truly wanted her.

She needed to get off this ship, needed some uninterrupted time to herself. Along with some Tanil-free air to breathe. Yes, that was it, off the ship. Right now. But hell, there was nowhere to go other than out the airlock. Not a viable option.

Her stomach growled. She looked down at the offending part and snapped at it.

"What? I just fed you…" She paused to look at the crystal display on the con, "a measly four hours ago." It sounded ridiculous even to her own ears, knowing she needed to eat often to keep up with her body's metabolism. Her enhanced physique required a lot of protein and fluids to stay healthy. Damn it. There was no replicator in here. No head either. And she needed to pee.

Tensed for action, her fingers automatically wrapped around the pistol at her back as a light tap sounded against the palm sensor on the other side of the door. Tanil was trying to get in. Did he know she was in here? Why hadn't she heard him get out of bed? Sickbay was only thirty meters away. Oh. She'd set her audio filter on max. Geesh.

"Scharsi? You in there?"

She didn't answer, willing him to go away just as a fresh but potently male fragrance trickled through the ceiling's air vent and tickled her nose, like smoke drifting underneath a door. Dark. Pungent. Almost savory. Mmmm, Gods, he smelled so good.

Snap out of it, damn it. You can't have him, so get over it. Then again, uh, why can't you have him? Shut up, shut up, shut up.

Besides, most men saw her as a conquest, a fear to be exorcised or something, wondering if they could survive a night with a female Super Soldier. Tanil didn't seem like the asshole type, but then again, what did she really know about this man?

Other than the fact that he sends your blood pressure through the top of your head?

Yeah, other than that.

Adjusting her hearing, she listened to him retreat and head off to the left. On silent feet, she exited the bridge, then locked it behind her. Not bothering to take the lift, she headed for the narrow stairs down to the second level. A good workout would do her good. Maybe she could sweat the lust away. If not, the airlock might start looking pretty good after all.

Chapter Four

Tanil had awoken to a dimly lit room.

Without moving a muscle, he'd surveyed his surroundings and took stock of his body at the same time. While he'd slept, Scharsi had removed the feeds, and disabled and removed the dome. The sides of the med-tech that kept him from moving around too much had retracted into the unit so it looked like a plain ordinary bed, though a narrow one. He'd sat up slowly, let the cool sheets slide down his chest and pool at his groin as he swung his legs over the side. It still amazed him how he'd come to be here, and that Scharsi had brought him aboard, stripped and hoisted him into the medical device without any aid, SS or not.

He'd sat on the edge of the bunk examining the barely scarred skin just below his left pectoral when the cabin door slid open. Scharsi had walked in, looked him up and down, taking in his bared skin in a slow visual caress. Gods, that expression in her honeyed eyes had scorched him from the inside out. He missed feeling the heat of that gaze when, with a shy smile on her luscious lips, she'd lowered her lashes, walked over to the replicator and spoke in that candy-smooth voice of hers.

"Male tactical gear. Generic size seventeen. Foot size: relative. All black. Include personal accessories in synthsilk." Then without another word, she'd turned and hightailed it right out the door.

Rising from his bunk, Tanil was more than pleased that his legs seemed to support him just fine. The woman had done a damn good job of programming the med-tech to repair his wounds.

He stepped close to the med console and was even more impressed. It appeared she'd done all the settings manually. One wrong guess on his metabolism and he might not have made it through alive. She'd even ordered him a toxin flush while he'd been healing, so at least he didn't smell like a man who'd been flat on his back for days.

How many days had it been anyway? Two? Four?

After a few shuffled steps, Tanil whirled around at a hissing sound behind him. It was only the med-tech's cot as it pulled back into the wall for storage. Gods, he was jumpy. But hell, he'd recently been almost assassinated, so guess he had a good reason for the nerves.

Better pull it together or your death could become more than just a rumor, Tan.

Gods, he was stiff and sore, but breathing, so no complaints. As he dragged his clothes onto his body, he wondered what had been going through Scharsi's mind when she'd exited so quickly. Did she find him repulsive? He didn't really think so, but her hasty exit gave him pause.

After eating a brownish-gray patty of what was probably some kind of protein filler laced with vitamins, courtesy of the replicator in the medical bay, Tanil approached the door and it slid open without a palm print or retinal scan. He stepped over the threshold and glanced up and down the quiet hallway. Since no one ran to slap restraints on him, he decided to take a little tour. He'd have to keep it short his first day out of bed. And as long as he didn't actually touch anything, he should be able to make his way around without ending up on his Gen8 host's shit list.

So far Scharsi had been more than gracious. Had even agreed to let him tag along on her trip to wherever she was going. No amount of pushing caused her to spill the beans, so he'd just have to trust that she wasn't delivering him to an Amalgamation prison hulk or worse — out the airlock.

Thankfully, she believed him to be no threat, but the woman made it clear she'd snap his neck at the first sign of treachery. Tanil didn't blame her for remaining somewhat reserved with him, though he'd shared all the information he could think of during each of her visits to his bed.

To his bed…now that sounded like a decadent proposition.

Since she believed he had nothing to do with her best friend's death, perhaps she could believe he truly found her desirable. Once this madness was over and done with, he'd like nothing more than a bit of peace and quiet holed up somewhere with Scharsi. He didn't know her well, but of one thing he was sure-the woman was a Gen8 to the bone. Skilled in combat yet with a sense of humanity and honor that even most humans lacked.

But she wasn't quite human, was she?

No, this woman was more, much more than even many of her supposedly advanced comrades. The contrast between Scharsi and the crazy-assed Gen10s he'd worked with was like

night and day. Where Scharsi had chosen to care
for him, a dying stranger covered with the scent
of a recently killed friend, a Gen10 would have
seen to it that he got as close to death as possible,
then interrogated him until he'd passed from
this plane to the next. Though it probably killed
her to be patient with him, Scharsi asked him
about his role in Carl's death and actually
listened to his answers. A Gen10 would have
told him what his role had been regardless of
whether it was true or not. And as for the info
he'd gathered on the IMF and their sick
experiments? A Gen10 would have seen it as a
good opportunity to serve their Amalgamation
masters. But not Scharsi. She was appalled,
angry and primed for revenge.

Yet revenge meant battle and battles always
held the possibility of death. One thought of the
woman in danger tightened Tanil's gut with
anxiety. But the thought of seeing her kick ass
and take names? Damn, it turned him on like a
high voltage switch!

Admiring the layout of the ship, Tanil let his
mind wander from thoughts of the sexy Scharsi,
to payback on the assholes who'd shot him, to
bringing down the Amalgamation, then all the
way back to Scharsi again. Absently rubbing the

small pink spot on his chest that used to be a laser rifle wound, he explored the main deck of the surprisingly roomy vessel. Interesting. The floors were blackish gray and coated with a rubbery substance that had a nice grip to it. Even if the floor was wet it would be difficult to slip on it. Very smart.

Spread out along the walls were jumper seats embedded between the metal girders that made up the frame of the ship. Anyone walking the halls could strap in if the vessel hit any unexpected bumps. Strange, since the crew consisted of a single female. The walls held what looked like covered storage spaces, but not wanting to be too nosey, he left them alone.

He passed rooms and niches with all manner of components, communications gear, computer switches and more buttons and panels than he knew what to do with.

The bottom of his stomach did a strange kind of flip when he caught sight of the one place he hadn't seen yet. The bridge. He approached and placed his hand on the sensor. Locked. No surprise there.

"Scharsi? You in there?" he called. A light tap on the metal of the threshold. "Shar?" No answer. He wondered where she'd gone off to.

His feet carried him past a half-galley with a single small table and two chairs. A bit further down the hall, he discovered Scharsi's quarters. Surprisingly wide-open quarters.

Unable to resist, Tanil stepped inside and took a quick look around. Hmm. They were sparse and said nothing of the woman who occupied them. Other than a few black tactical synthsilk shirts and pants in the small storage unit, there seemed to be nothing personal here. Nothing except her scent. It was faint, which made sense considering they'd only been on the ship a few days. Faint, but there none the less.

Tanil felt welcome and out of place at the same time. Backing up he quickly left the room and moved along.

Where was that woman? He'd surely covered every bit of this ship, but hadn't seen her anywhere. What started out as an exploration of his surroundings had turned into a hunting expedition. The thought brought him up short. There was no real reason to find Scharsi…other than the fact he enjoyed her presence. He didn't need anything. He wasn't in pain. Wasn't even hungry. Well, at least not for food. But her presence had become necessary and he had no idea why.

Moving on, he discovered the lift down to the second floor. His skin itched as he passed the full-sized head complete with shower and commode. But what really caught and held him was a full galley complete with the most modern replicator unit and a cold storage unit stocked to the hilt with, to his surprise, many of his favorite foods.

He snagged a lillee fruit from the cold storage, passed through the galley, swung around the corner and came to a dead stop. The fruit he'd been snacking on almost fell from his mouth. Instead he swallowed it quickly and thumped his chest, trying not to choke since he'd forgotten to finish chewing it.

A little ways down the well-lit hallway with her head more than three and a half meters from the floor, hanging from the ceiling like some sculpted work of art, was Scharsi.

Holy shit!

The woman did sit ups completely upside down, suspended from an inversion bar overhead. He stood transfixed and watched her stomach muscles bunch and release. Watched the sweat glisten across her midsection and down her back. Watched the strong fingers interlaced behind her neck as she lifted her torso up and let it back down again in smooth practiced moves.

Her little workout clothes looked painted on. The fabric flowed over her skin as if she'd been dipped in it. The midriff tank covered her breasts…and that was all. A pair of shorts in a stretchy material that didn't quite look like synthsilk covered her thighs, and on her feet were a pair of black, soft-soled tactical three-quarter shank boots.

She looked lethal. And delicious. And just like that, his cock took notice and his balls danced around in his pants.

"You missed one," she called down to him in between reps.

"Huh?" He was too busy watching the curve of her ass to hear what she'd said. "What?"

"I said," she said on a deep breath in, "you missed one." Controlled breath out.

Damn, look at all those sleek fucking muscles, all toned and glistening. This woman even sweats sexy.

"Damn," he whispered. "You are one sexy woman." Skin so smooth and dark it reminded him of his favorite liquor.

She seemed to stiffen the second the words left his lips, but continued to lift her torso.

Perhaps she hadn't heard him. He was several steps away, barely breathing and certainly speaking lower than a whisper. Then again, it was easy to forget she was SS. He'd worked with them forever and knew they had hearing so acute it bordered on sonar, Godsdammit. Then again, perhaps she had her auditory filter turned on and really couldn't hear him at all. Wickedness reared its head and Tanil decided a little experiment was in order.

As quiet as he could, he stood there and whispered to his lovely host. "If your auditory filter is turned off, then you'll hear every word I say. We've been on this ship a few days now and every time you come to see me in medical, I fight with my body not to get hard. You're so fucking beautiful. So gorgeous. In spite of your recent loss, I find myself wishing you were in my bed. Perhaps we can love each other's pain away."

That was the sappiest damn thing he'd ever said. Yet he meant every word. Gods, he must be crazy. Just as he turned to walk away to go regain some of his pride, a barely perceptible thud registered in Tanil's brain. He abandoned his musings and turned back toward the sound.

Scharsi stood in front of him toweling off her gorgeous body. If she'd heard him, she gave no indication of it.

"Hey, you okay? Do you need to go back into the med-tech?" she asked, her brows pulled down into a concerned frown.

"What? Uh, no. I'm fine."

"You don't look fine. And your breathing is somewhat erratic. And…" she said saucily over her shoulder, "my hearing is so keen I could pick up your heartbeat from across the room. Unsteady."

Was that her way of saying she'd heard what he said? But for the life of him he couldn't think of a single thing to say. So he just stood there watching her watch him.

"What? Your expression is a bit odd," she declared with a tilt of her lovely head.

Well, he was tired from spending so much time exploring when he'd only been one day out of the med-tech, but Tanil was sure the look on his face was more from trying to keep from drooling over the beauty of a woman than any true fatigue.

"Anyway, I said you missed one."

Tanil was more confused than ever. Why was she covering up her lovely breasts with a shirt? And what the hell was she talking about?

"Missed what?"

"You've been all over my ship, but you haven't seen it all. You missed a room."

How the hell did she know that? He hadn't seen hide nor hair of her for the last two hours until now. "I did? Okay. What was it?"

"The armory."

"Armory? What the hell kind of vessel is this?"

"This ship isn't called the Futsuka-shi, Second Death, for nothing," she grinned.

Gods, it was devastating, that smile of hers. Bright enough to melt every meter of glacial ice on the entire planet of Lelo. Beguiling enough to bring a man to his knees. Literally…where he could bury his face between her legs and dine. Suddenly Tanil wanted nothing more than to see Scharsi with that smile on her face more often. Tossing a towel over one shoulder, she headed toward a panel in the wall that looked like any other piece of synthsteel. "You, my new friend, are aboard a war class cruiser with military grade weaponry, including stealth, modified laser cannons and half-sized plasma cannons. And lots of other interesting weapons."

"But I thought this was a medical ship?"

"Used to be a medical ship."

With that she placed her palm over a certain

spot as high as she could reach and the panel slid back and to the side with a quiet hiss. Tanil followed her inside where she pushed one of five unmarked buttons. The panel slid closed and they began to move slowly downward.

"Holy shit. There's another deck? How?" Tanil sputtered.

"Carl and I kept this baby in a private hanger on Ukure. It's such a small, obsolete planet and so close to the Reptilios border, we don't get much traffic other than the illegal kind. This ship's been meticulously cared for and upgraded over the years. As for the how, pirates don't ask questions. Pay 'em and you can get just about anything, including bootlegged munitions and equipment. Ukure is close enough to the outlooks to take advantage of such things. We're actually in a hidden room in the cargo bay, but you can't see or get to it through the cargo bay. You can only get in through the private lift upstairs."

The door snicked open and he stood there in awe as the Gods' personal weapons room opened to him in all its glory. He followed her inside and gawked at the latest killing machines, complete with bells and whistles. Wow. He'd always been a sucker for a really cool gun.

"Why are you showing me this?" he wondered aloud.

"Because." She crowded into his space, probably trying to gauge whether he would back up, but intimidated he was not. Scared? Not even close. Horny? Beyond belief.

"I've decided to trust you, Tanil. Completely."

They were toe-to-toe, with Tanil barely five centimeters taller than her. Her lips were at the perfect height for kissing. And he wanted it. Wanted her with a hunger so strong it filled up all of the available space inside him. Every nerve, every cell. Every breath. Holy hell, what had she put in his meds to make him so hard up for her? Last he checked there was nothing other than Carnelian Tears that made a man want to give up any and everything to attach himself by the hip to a woman. Only Carnelian royalty had the ability to excrete the Tears and only during sex, and even that was rumored to be a myth.

So what was it about Scharsi? Perhaps the woman was simply potent. In spite of the fact she was a fighting machine, sensuality oozed from her pores like thick honeyed syrup. Gods, he wanted to dip his finger in it and lick it off for starters.

Tanil didn't back up or allow his gaze to leave hers. If anything, the urge to be closer hit him square between the shoulder blades and moved him forward before he knew it. Toe-to-toe wasn't close enough. He put his feet outside hers, leaned in and let the heat of her breasts scorch his chest, urge him to rub up against her like a feline would its mate.

Confusion clouded her features.

"Why?" she asked on a whisper.

He knew what she wanted to know, but didn't have an answer. Actually, he had no idea why he felt so compelled to kiss her. To taste her. He only knew that every time he looked at her, every time he caught her scent, the need to curl around her body and hold her close rose up inside his soul. Strange. He couldn't recall ever feeling this attracted to a woman in at least, hell he wasn't sure when, if ever.

With a tilt of his head, his lips found hers.

She didn't touch him, but didn't push him away either. What she did was open to him, let him lead her in the dance as their mouths melded until the heat of it rivaled the warmest, wettest, most humid spring day on Trescalane's Southern Tulane, that beautiful island city in the Southern Hemisphere in the middle of the Sea of

Doss. Refreshing and naturally beautiful. In a word, potent.

For certain, Scharsi was nothing like the monster the IMF painted all Super Soldiers to be. And she was definitely nothing like the sadistic Gen10's he'd worked with in the past. Those nutjobs were everything rumors claimed them to be and then some. They felt no pain, no remorse, no emotion. Their goal in life was to compare kills with their comrades in a game of who's-the-better-killer.

Scharsi didn't seem the bloodthirsty or vindictive type. But then he couldn't really tell. She seemed determined to keep herself locked away, tightly controlled at all times. Yet she'd let her guard down just long enough for him to catch the sorrow and grief lurking behind her eyes every now and again, though she always quickly recovered. No surprise considering the stock she hailed from—Generation Eight Super Soldier. Calculating, brilliant, expert tacticians, but not the most dependable creations, considering their sense of honor. Too moral to suit the purposes of the Amalgamation.

Scharsi. The woman oozed sensuality, but wore her heart on her sleeve, or at least that's what he believed.

And she kissed him like she couldn't get enough.

* * * * *

What was she supposed to do? This was a drastically unfamiliar circumstance. Should she allow Tanil to continue to kiss her? Or should she punch him in the gut to make him back up? No, that wouldn't be right. He wasn't trying to hurt her. But he was a stranger, or rather an acquaintance of mere days, most of which he'd spent in the med-tech unable to move anything except his mouth and his wrist.

Yet in the short time Tanil had been on her ship, he'd given her more details on the inner workings of the Amalgamation than she could have obtained in a lifetime on her own. The man had dropped the inside scoop on some scary operations that were supposed to be rumors and sick legends. And she used to work for those bastards? Worse, she'd been bred in their labs, created by them.

Curiosity overcame the fog of passion. Her open palms landed gently on his once-battered chest and eased him away.

"Why aren't you afraid of me?"

"If you wanted to hurt me, you've had plenty of opportunity. On the other hand, when you look at me I get all achy inside, as if there's a Scharsi sized hole in my chest that you fit perfectly into. Makes me wonder what else fits perfectly. Gods, woman…" He nuzzled her cheek with his, rubbing along her jaw. "I know it sounds crazy, maybe even corny, but you call to me, both mind and body."

He moved closer. A stone-hard erection pressed into her stomach. It had been ages since she'd let an aroused man press up against her. But where was all this going? Her spine snapped as rigid as a steel tie rod when she realized that she had no idea.

Turn off the analytics, Scharsi. He's horny. You're horny. Don't turn this into a permanent mating or something.

Hell, she wouldn't know a long-term thing if it cold-cocked her in the face anyway. Duty, followed by the need to stay alive and on the run, had allowed her nothing more than boring hand jobs delivered by none other than herself. Oh joy.

Then Tanil kissed her again. Her lips, her chin, along her jaw. Gods, it felt so good. His mouth was warm, firm. His touch, sure and confident.

Sigh. She'd always loved an assertive man.

Correction—had always imagined what it would be like to have a self-assured lover. Scharsi hadn't experienced many, other than those in her former military unit, and they were technically off limits.

A light nip along her bottom lip snatched a gasp out of her. And Tanil wasted no time taking advantage of it. He slipped his tongue along hers to tangle with it. Mmmm, lillee fruit. Oh yes, Tanil was now her favorite flavor.

That's it, girlfriend. Just enjoy the moment. It's been ages since you've even had a moment, remember?

Thoughts flashed back to the one man who'd been her constant company for the past seven years. But he'd been her best friend, not her lover. Carl.

That was all it took to snap her out of the sensual haze Tanil had carefully cultivate around them both.

Her heart pounded a cadence against her ribs. The allure of being held in a man's arms, this man's arms, fought against the thoughts pounding inside her skull. And then it came to the rescue—knee-buckling guilt. It slammed to the forefront of her mind and wiped away any remaining thoughts of sexual bliss.

With a subtle shift of her body, Scharsi put a bit of distance between her and Tanil. His hands fell away from her torso as he followed her movements closely.

He must have read her body language like a pro because he backed up a step. Head tilted in concern, his expressive brown eyes took in the tight lines around her mouth, the deep dip of her brows as they formed a frown.

"Shar? What's wrong?"

His head tilted to the side as his gaze tried to capture hers. Her chin dropped to rest against her chest as it rose and fell with each deep breath.

She couldn't, wouldn't look at him.

Instead she walked away. Every step felt as if she slogged through knee deep mud left behind after the flooding rains in the jungles of Earth.

Chapter Five

Later that day, or perhaps it was night—it was difficult to tell in the blackness of space—Scharsi's guilt from the role she'd played in Carl's death carved an empty cavern in the pit of her stomach. Sure it had been Carl's idea to steal her from the lab, but she'd chosen to stay with him. Perhaps if she hadn't he'd still be alive today.

Then there was her body's reaction to Tanil, both unexpected and almost as guilt inducing as Carl's death. Scharsi had never had any sexual desire for Carl, nor he for her. Yet he'd risked everything for her and paid the ultimate price for it. Yet here she was practically panting like a Pyaw randwulf in heat for the man who'd been sent to capture the only person who'd ever looked out for her, cared for her simply because it was the right thing to do. Not because he'd been ordered to or threatened into it.

And this heat between her and her guest, it just wasn't logical. Sex was a simple biological function. It had always been a detached activity that did little more than send her heart rate up for a few sweaty minutes, and only when arranged by the Military Sciences Lab task masters, of course. While the male SS were occasionally given leave to pursue their pleasures where they wished, the females were monitored much more closely. Something about testing to see if their altered DNA precluded the possibility of procreation. Sometimes the bastards even attached monitors to her and whatever partner had been chosen and sanitized like a lab rat just for her. They recorded pulse, breathing, muscle contraction, hell, they even recorded how long it took her to come. Thankfully their window of opportunity was short since they could only conduct the idiotic experiments during the few days between her yearly fertility inoc.

Sex between fellow soldiers was punishable by whatever means the MSL or IMF felt like doling out at the time, anything from running until you hurled up your guts to re-indoctrination or even termination. And while Scharsi enjoyed the idea of sex, recognized her body's need for closeness to another person, the fact that she'd been conditioned not to want it bristled. Perhaps that's what had kept her shut off from others, including Carl. She was sure that if she'd wanted sex he would have given it to her. After all, Carl was — had been — a healthy, handsome male of breeding age who did manage to entertain his fair share of occasional visitors when he thought she wasn't home.

Well, at least one of us was getting some. She almost snickered at the thought.

This, this thing with Tanil was different. It dipped beneath the skin and lodged in her blood. And too damn intense to deal with while her mind should be on catching those responsible for Carl's murder. Her honor demanded it. Her conscience required it.

But hell if she could resist Tanil's touch. And that ratcheted up the guilt to a whole new level.

Now all she had to do was figure out what she felt guilty about. She once again left the locked bridge behind and made her way back down to the lowest level of the ship. A good workout would do her good.

"I thought I'd find you in here."

Even with all the weapons within arm's reach of Tanil, Scharsi didn't fear for her safety. If necessary she could have Tanil neutralized in a very painful submission hold on the floor before he could grab a weapon off the shelf and remove the safety. What warmed her clear through her mind and soul was the fact that he didn't fear for his safety.

"So what's your specialty?" Tanil asked, running his fingers over a black-and-gray laser rifle with a sniper scope. It was a very nice gun. And the way his hands glided over the smooth finish was nothing short of seductive. And now a single digit eased it's way through the trigger hole and gently eased the tip along the inside of it.

"My specialty is, uh…" What the hell had she been about to say? Okay, deep breath. And stop watching him touch that gun! "It's hand-to-hand combat and knife fighting, among other things."

"Knife fighting? You mean with blades? Who uses blades anymore?"

"That's exactly why it's so effective. People don't expect it." Scharsi whipped one of her favorite daggers from the shelf to her left—a specialized Icsantheze blade modified especially for her. The wicked blade was half its typical size at thirty centimeters from tip to blade instead of the usual sixty-six. Easier to hide in the specialized holster made to lie low and diagonally across her back underneath whatever coat or jacket she wore.

The pale green streaks forged into the golden blade shimmered as she snatched it off the rack and flipped it back and forth across the back of her hand until it was a blur in motion.

"Damn, woman, you are impressive."

Impressive? Not scary? Or intimidating? What about "manly"? So he really wasn't afraid of her? Huh.

The next instant he was in her face, literally. His lips moved over hers in a kiss so blatantly scorching she melted on contact.

"Gods, Scharsi, I can't seem to keep my hands off you. That one kiss earlier has haunted me all day, tempted me to find you and take another."

Scharsi turned her head away from his ravenous lips, her soul soaked in pain. She knew her rejection hurt Tanil, but she wasn't rejecting him. Not really. It was more a rejection of her own desires.

"Tanil, I shouldn't feel this way."

"Why?"

"It's just that Carl…well, he. I mean, we…"

Her words stumbled over one another taking her aback. Trained in analytics and reasoning, Scharsi had been groomed to be well versed and well spoken. Yet here she stood with her gut dancing around her middle while she struggled to get a full sentence out of her mouth.

She stiffened when Tanil backed off chasing her lips with his and simply gathered her into a close embrace.

"Hey, we don't have to talk about it." There was no doubt he meant it. And those eight words of his made her spill all her deepest feelings.

"I need to talk about it. It's killing me," she whispered against his neck.

"If you're sure then I'll gladly listen," he encouraged gently. And at that moment Scharsi experienced a bone-deep revelation — she knew she had to be completely honest with this man. To tell him everything that was in her heart and mind. Something she'd never done with another living person.

"Carl and I were best friends, you know that. We lived in the same house. The folks on Ukure assumed we were married and we never disabused them of the notion. But we never had sex." Why was it so important to make that clear? Hmm. She'd examine that later. "We loved each other, but we weren't in love. Yet he loved me as deeply as any man could. I know that if I'd pursued more than friendship with him he would have gladly taken me. But now I'll never be able to show him how much I really cared for him. I'll never be able to hold him again. Or eat his terrible cooking again. Or just sit and enjoy his company again."

"It's okay, baby."

Baby? Another first. Her life had been amazingly void of endearments.

"But you don't understand, Tanil. No one will ever understand."

"I do understand. You feel guilty that Carl is dead and you're alive. You feel guilty because he gave up ever finding true love the day he stole you from those labs and placed himself on the IMF's bounty watch list. And it's eating you alive that his life could have been so much different if he'd never saved yours."

Yep, he'd summed it up succinctly enough, but the unexpected clog of tears in her throat wouldn't allow her to speak.

"What, you think you were supposed to lie to him? Tell him you felt something that you didn't? Have sex with him because you felt obligated? From what I know of Dr. Sabbo, he was an honorable man, a man of great courage.

Courageous enough to defy the most powerful war machine throughout the galaxies for the last two hundred years. He took on the Amalgamation itself when he took you. And he deserved honesty from you, not a bunch of lies just to soothe your conscience."

Ouch. But true...

"He would want you to be happy, Scharsi. Isn't that true?"

All she could do was nod.

"You can tell me I'm right now or later. But it won't change the facts, Shar. There is nothing wrong with you being attracted to me as I am to you. Nothing wrong with you wanting me. And I doubt Dr. Sabbo would want you steeped in guilt like this over something that was out of your control in regard to his death. Hell, it was even out of my control and I was fucking sent to get him. Now look at me."

Gentle fingers formed a vee as he held her chin between his thumb and forefinger. But she couldn't do it. Couldn't meet his eyes. Twisting away from his grip Scharsi sought to look at something else, anything but those soft, amber eyes. She couldn't stand to see the truth in them.

But Tanil was a stubborn bastard. The more she tried to twist away, the firmer his grip became until she knew she'd either hurt him or herself if she continued the silliness. And it was definitely silly. The acknowledgement almost brought a smirk to her lips. Almost. At least she had some control around this man. Not much, but some.

"I said look at me, Scharsi." There was the command in his voice. That masculine dip of a half octave that rippled under her kneecaps like a gentle wave at low tide.

"Let me love you. Let me love the hurt away."

It sounded good, but he didn't even know her. Love? What the hell was that? Scharsi had no idea, at least not in the "couple" sense of the word. But damn, it didn't change the way the bottom fell out of her gut when he moved in close once again.

This time Tanil's kiss was soft. So sweet it drew out the tears she'd fought so hard to contain. But soon enough the sweet became spicy, and spicy became hot until her skin heated just enough to make her ache. Just enough to make her imagine the streak of tears on her cheeks evaporating with the heat.

Breaking the kiss, Scharsi's head fell back and met the metal rack Tanil had backed her

---

against without her even noticing. Then his tongue dipped into the hollow at the center of her collarbone.

"No, wait. Let me shower first. I'm all sweaty." After leaving him earlier she'd gone to the bridge instead of washing up from her workout. Now she regretted it. But there was no way she would go to him all funky.

He murmured against her skin. "But you taste so good."

A neat-freak by nature, Scharsi was surprised his words turned her on rather than grossed her out. In fact, Carl used to deliberately clutter up her room just to get a rise out of her. And every time she'd growled at him for mussing up her space he'd remind her that her file claimed she was particular about her appearance and surroundings. If anyone came looking for her, they'd never believe she lived there. He'd been right.

"But..." Tanil whispered against her skin. "If it makes you more comfortable to shower, go ahead. I'll find you in a bit."

"A bit?" Her eyes were still closed, arms twined around his neck, and she hadn't moved at all though he'd backed away.

"Yes. Seven minutes. Does that count as a

bit?"

She laughed. Couldn't help it and was surprised at the sound that bubbled up out of her chest. She stood there and marveled.

"You're down to six and a half minutes, beautiful."

"Fine. I'm going already." Then that same laugh pushed up from beneath the surface and burst out of her chest as she headed toward the head for a shower.

Washed and wrapped in a towel, Scharsi headed up to her quarters. Nervous anticipation rode her hard about what would happen there, especially since she'd deliberately taken much longer than the time needed for a quick shower. And her question was answered when instinct brought her up short in the wide hallway just steps from her room. Tanil was there. She could feel him.

A warm hand landed gently on both shoulders and she was pulled back into a wide, hard and surprisingly naked chest.

"A bit presumptuous, aren't you?" she asked.

His answer sent her head into outer space. Pun intended.

"Not presumptuous. Sure. I couldn't wait another second to feel your skin against mine, even if most of it is temporarily wrapped in a towel. And you're going the wrong way."

"Huh?" She wasn't so daft that she didn't know where her own quarters were.

"Turn around and go with me to the galley. Let's get you fed first. I plan to keep you busy for a while. Wouldn't do for you to faint on me."

"Faint? I've never fainted in my life."

"There's always a first time."

Holy shit! He was serious.

* * * * *

He'd teased her mercilessly during dinner. Having surprised her with the knowledge that he could actually cook more than dehydrated military rations, Tanil was pretty proud of the fresh foods he'd prepared as a result of raiding her cold storage. He'd ended the meal with a shot of fruity Tropicure for the both of them.

And Scharsi was as potent as the liquor he'd served up. And he couldn't wait to taste her, to see if she was as sweet, whether she would coat his tongue, then burn him on the way down.

Thoughts tumbled around in his head but he kept his mouth closed. After all, he could sense her uncertainty, and the last thing he wanted was to say something stupid and chase her away.

Instead he held her hand in a gentle grip and led her to her quarters in silence. The door slid open with a quiet hiss. She froze at the threshold. Raising his hands slowly so as not to startle her, Tanil let his fingers dip into the tense muscles of her neck and shoulders. A few seconds passed, then he stepped closer.

"Invite me in?"

A slight turn and her gaze locked with his.

For a moment, Tanil was struck by the sheer, raw beauty of the woman. Words stuck in his throat as he moved around her body to stand before her.

"I have to touch you, Shar." Gently he placed his hands on either side of her head and guided her into his kiss. Just before their lips touched he stilled, looking deeper into the light brown of her muted honey-colored eyes.

And there it was—fear. Stark, barely leashed. Something he doubted she had much experience with. Her facial features gave away nothing. Every muscle in her body appeared relaxed and uncommonly still. Yet her eyes told it all. She was terrified. The question—what was she afraid of? Certainly not him in a physical sense. Scharsi was built like a damn prison hulk—strong enough to contain the meanest, baddest criminal in the 'verse. If she wanted out, there was nothing he could do to stop her. They both knew that.

Sex? Sure, she could handle that. He was, after all, former Interplanetary Military. He knew all about the SS program. Scharsi would have been trained to be good at it like she was groomed to be good at everything else. But attraction? Now that was another matter altogether. And from what he knew of the rigorous and brutal training that all SS went through, attraction was not something that was allowed. Ever. She would be woefully unprepared to deal with it.

Unable to resist, Tanil drew his thumb over a plump bottom lip, teasing the flesh until she gently bit down. He shook his head and smiled. Not a plastic, perfectly practiced spreading of his lips, but a genuine smile that he felt clear down to the depths of his soul.

He knew exactly what she would do next— attempt to regain control.

"Not happening, Shar."

"What?" she asked. Her tongue now followed his thumb back and forth across her mouth.

"You don't get to be in charge. Not tonight." Or any other night. "But I promise I won't fuck you without your full consent and cooperation. Ever."

She started to protest, he could feel it in the tightening muscles in the center of her back as he moved a hand to gently stroke up and down her spine.

"You get to be a woman right now. No need to be a soldier. Let me take care of you, even just for a little while. Give me complete control of your release. Promise me."

"I... Okay. Tonight."

A world of promise rang in those few words. Get it right, Tan, or you may not get another chance. Why this was so important to him, he hadn't a clue. But it didn't matter. This woman was willing to give him something that she'd obviously never given any man. Ever. And he would not fuck it up. If he had to bite off his tongue to make this good for her, he would.

Backing up several steps, he eased her along with him until the backs of his knees hit the firm pad of her bunk. He sat, pulling her into his lap to straddle him with a knee on each side of his body.

"Just sit there. Let me kiss you."

Tanil's brain screamed for him to ravish her mouth. Instead he forced himself to deliver sweet kisses, then tempting and teasing caresses until his instinct, what little was left in his lust-filled head, told him she was ready for more.

Arms wrapped around his neck, she leaned fully into his body, chest to breast. The warmth of her skin seeped through her towel. Wait, why was she still wearing a towel?

Because you're so consumed with her mouth. And he was. She tasted of the lillee fruit they'd had with dinner, tart and sweet, a delicacy hard to come by and to be savored. Yes, she was lillee and exotic sensual spice that seemed to simply be her natural flavor. Gods it was addictive.

Soft little moans accompanied a deep intake of breath when he broke the kiss to create a path of nips down one side of her neck. The press of her lovely breasts through the towel left a sizzle in its wake as her spine arched and slithered from side to side. Closer. She needs to be closer. Let her feel your skin.

Tanil peeled Scharsi's towel away, baring her beautiful body. The valley between her lovely breasts held a light sheen of sweat that made her dark candied skin glow with health. He wanted to lick a path through it.

So he did.

With one hand planted firmly in the center of her back and the other encircling a luscious breast, Tanil lowered his head and feasted.

"Aah," she panted. "Oh, that's good." Then bit her lip as if she wasn't supposed to say any more.

Tanil lifted his head and waited for her to realize that he'd stopped. This was important, more important than anything he'd had to muddle through in a long while.

"Scharsi, you feel so good against me. It's been a long time since I've loved a woman." Love. Hmm. He'd have to analyze that later, but it felt like the word could come to have more meaning than he usually allocated to it. "I want to make you feel good, to fall apart."

She opened her mouth to say something, he cut across her words.

"This isn't the IMF. No one is going to tell you that you can't enjoy this. Want this. I'm responsible for your pleasure tonight. And I won't allow you to hold back on me."

That said, he lowered his mouth again and licked the underside of a firm breast. He liked her breasts. They were just the right size for her. He didn't think it would have made sense for her to have huge voluptuous breasts amidst all that muscle. No, these breasts weren't overly big, but firm, just about a handful. And sensitive as hell.

That one lick sent her ass squirming. And his cock not only took notice, but began to voice its impatient opinion on the matter of not being inside her.

"Your nipples are getting hard. Do you like this?" he asked. Then proceeded to nip and suck the ripe little berries until her moans became gasps, then fervent demands.

"Oh Gods, please. Please…"

"But you didn't answer my question. Do you like this?"

"Yes, damn it. I like it."

"Do you like it a bit rougher, baby?"

"Yes. Rougher. Harder."

So he proceeded to give her more. More sucking, moving from one breast to the other and back again. More nipping. Tanil noticed that she reacted more to the rougher twists of her nipples, the more ardent nips on her skin. Not as rough as he'd like to venture, but that was for another time.

Barely coming up for breath, Tanil took both breasts in his hands and stuffed his face between them. Scharsi's hands tightened in his hair. That little edge of pain ratcheted up his pleasure like a shot of tryptocain directly into a vein.

"Gods, woman, the way you get to me is insane."

Again, that damn stiffening of her spine, like she wasn't sure whether she wanted him to eat her alive, or back off instead. Then she relaxed and went all boneless on him as if she'd made a decision to just roll with it.

"Mmm, good choice, baby." Tanil lay back and dragged Scharsi up his body. She reached for his cock.

"No. Not tonight." If the woman touched him now, the thin shell over his enforced calm would crack. He was already having a tough time reining in his baser instincts. There was no way he could afford to let her strip his control. Gods knows he'd never be able to get it back. And that simply wouldn't do. At least not this first time together. But there would be others. He was sure of it.

"Let me taste you." Pointing to his mouth, he said, "Sit right here, baby. Come give me that pretty pussy."

Giving her no time to reconsider, Tanil took hold of a thigh in each hand and slid Scharsi up and along his body until her tender folds were positioned perfectly. His tongue and lips went to work, easing along the sensitive inner labia to tease the weeping entrance to her center, fluttering just out of reach of where he knew she wanted him most.

"Spread yourself, Scharsi."

Without hesitation, her fingers settled on either side of her budding clit and eased the soft lips away. Tanil got a clear view of the little bundle of nerves, a pink treat in the midst of succulent cacao skin.

Again the unmistakable hint of lillee fruit was there. It occurred to Tanil that she enjoyed the delicacy. It would explain why there was quite a cache in her cooling unit. And he'd make sure she always had some. Her body's natural flavor was savory, and the hint of lillee only added to the addictive flavor — like the heavens dusted with star flowers.

Tanil noted the spot that made the breath catch in Scharsi's throat with an audible gasp, the exact pressure of his tongue on her clit that sent her thigh muscles into a light spasm as if she tried to control her body's reaction to his touch. Oh yeah, he made note of it all right. Then touched her there again and again until the real Scharsi came out to play.

The uninhibited and sensual being that lurked beneath the surface of the warrior had arrived. And declared her presence with fervor.

* * * * *

With gentle swirls of his tongue along the dip between the major and minor labia, Tanil pushed her gently toward overload. Soft licks followed by firm presses kept her just off balance enough to allow herself to tip into a sensual haze.

"Reach down and spread yourself for me, baby."

She did…or rather she started to, but snatched her hand back and away from her sex. It felt so good, so damn deliciously decadent to have this man's mouth on her. So why the hesitation? It wasn't as if she'd never had sex before. Sure it had been a good stretch since her last fulfilling encounter, but that was no reason for the sudden shyness. So what…?

Tanil didn't give her time to think about it. The moment she moved to do what he asked and her fingers made contact with the silken skin of her sex, he slipped a single strong digit into her moist heat. Just one was all it took to send her inner muscles into an involuntary tremor. He eased it out, slid up just a bit to the underside of her clit but didn't stroke it. The anticipation of him actually touching the little bundle of nerves set her teeth on edge. 'Do it. Do it!' she cried silently. Instead, he returned to make a deeper dive into her sex. It sent a strengthening ripple through her walls just as he moved back out again to tease the sensitive flesh at her entrance.

The teasing would drive her nuts if she allowed it to continue. But what were her options? Turn the tables on him? Nope. She'd given up that possibility the moment she'd agreed to this little tryst. The terms rang in her head as the heat spiraled in her body. Complete control of her release. Gods, what the hell had she been thinking?

Now two fingers parted her honeyed walls as his tongue licked and teased. Filled her without fulfilling her. A full lick from north to south sent her thoughts into a whirlwind. The analytical reasoning in her head was swallowed up by pure, unadulterated lust. Thighs spread wide, Scharsi's hips began a journey of their own and struck a rhythm with his shallow strokes.

More. Gods, she needed more.

Sweat began to bead behind her knees as the ever elusive orgasm hovered just out of reach.

"Oh Gods," she panted. Tried to hold the words back, but even her mouth was out of her control.

"You want this, Scharsi?" A muted cry, one she was sure she'd never made before, accompanied a fierce swivel of her hips as they chased his fingers around. "Say the words."

So, the man was into torture? Tuck that away for future use. But there was no heat behind the thought because all the warmth was pooled low in her belly and radiated through her pussy.

"Tell me," Tanil said. Sounded like the words were bitten off the tip of his tongue. The thought almost made her smile. Almost.

"I want it."

"How much?"

Her body stilled, muscles taut and tension filled. What did he want from her? She was already on fire. Already fighting the wave of acidic guilt attempting to wash over her will to move past Carl's demise. Already approaching the need to beg. Then it hit her square in the middle of her consciousness what the man was after. The truth. Plain and simple. So she let surface the soft female psyche she so often suppressed. Let it come up for air and tell this masculine prize exactly what she wanted.

"I want it, Tanil. I need to…please, I need to come." No shame. No regrets.

And then the man went to work. Feasted on her juicy folds until they throbbed. Thrust his fingers deeper, harder, longer.

"Oh yes, lick it. Lick it just like that."

She wasn't sure how the man managed to accomplish such an anatomically impossible feat, but Tanil curled his tongue around her clit, squeezed, released, then stroked in one smooth move. Curl, squeeze, release, stroke. Over and over until her hips chased his mouth, desperate to keep the contact.

"Yes! Yes! Oh my Gods!"

Her womb tightened to the point of pain before it exploded, pulsed and quivered.

He hadn't penetrated her, but it was certainly more than "almost" sex. She knew it, had experienced a deep connection before, during and after that breath-stealing climax.

And that was when she made the decision to never let it happen again. But when Tanil swept her into his arms and cradled her lovingly against his chest without asking her for anything in return for the blistering orgasm he'd given her, the decision unmade itself.

Chapter Six

As if thoughts of the woman made her appear, Scharsi stood at the door and said, "Be ready to debark in five minutes or you'll go naked. And you need to take this." She slipped a small yellow sphere into his palm.

"What is it?" Without hesitation, he popped it into his mouth and swallowed it down. Then wished he hadn't.

"It's going to make you sick as a dog."

Huh?

"I feel fine. Great, even."

"Yeah, but you're not expected where we're going. You need to have a reason to be with me, otherwise things could get…unpleasant. Trust me, your identity as an Amalgamation officer won't stay quiet for long. At least not with this group."

Tanil felt his eyes widen beneath the lids, though he forced a neutral expression.

"Before you even ask, no, I haven't told anyone who you are or where you're from," Scharsi assured. "But that doesn't change the fact that the place we're headed is in the

Hide no More

business of information. Without it they die, which means we die. And I think you've been close enough to death once already, don't you?"

Puh, no kidding. The spot on his chest had completely healed, but Tanil could swear it burned just then in remembrance of his brush with the ever after.

"So…" The word dragged on as Scharsi took in his state of undress…very slowly. When her gaze reached his cock, which happened to be growing harder by the second, a single pass of her tongue over her bottom lip made her appear to be contemplating. Tanil almost smiled at the appreciation with which she perused his bare skin, but his lips suddenly felt pulled in tight to his teeth. What a nasty feeling.

"Gods, you are such a complete package," she crooned.

Perhaps there was time for a taste? He took one step toward her and halted at her outstretched hand raised in the universal "stay" position. Hmm. His head felt somewhat thick and a bit tight too, just like his lips and teeth.

"Five minutes, stud. Definitely not enough time for what you, or rather your cock, has in mind. Besides, in exactly eight minutes you won't be too good for much of anything."

And just like that, Scharsi spun on silent tactically booted feet and disappeared through the open door.

In exactly five minutes, Tanil stood at the hatch with no doubt in his mind that Scharsi would indeed leave him to his fate if he were late. That included getting him off her ship in nothing but his skin, if need be.

* * * * *

The second the outramp lowered, Scharsi popped the external hatch. The unmistakable whirr of laser sidearms made the hair on her arms do a little wave. There was no fear, only the nurtured anticipation of battle from years of training. She could almost pump adrenaline on command. Damn handlers made sure of it.

"S24?"

Scharsi recognized the sexy-as-hell voice as the one she'd heard several times through her communications console during the flight here. She hadn't expected the spiked muss of dark hair nor the crystalline-blue eyes. Though she typically liked her males a bit less…scruffy, still the man attached to said voice did not disappoint. He wasn't dead-on-sight gorgeous, but handsome was definitely too light a word.

At a single nod of her head, "the voice"

stepped politely forward. Too bad the wolfish gleam in his eye gave away the nature beneath the cordial shell.

"I'm Sealy Garrison. We weren't expecting additional…guests."

"Neither was I," Scharsi quipped, barely cutting Tanil a glance. "He's a stray. Been in my med-tech for days. Could probably use a bit more time under care."

Tanil started to protest, then remembered their little chat just before debarkation. Not to mention the look she sent his way conveyed a wealth of meaning—shut up or else.

Considering the woman knew more about where they were than he did, Tanil clamped his mouth shut and stood there with what he hoped was a bored, though slightly ill expression.

"Medical attention, eh? And afterward, then what?" Sealy asked.

Tanil didn't like the way the other male's brow rose while his eyes practically stripped Scharsi where she stood. She seemed oblivious. No smile. No change in expression. Just chocolate perfection endowed with deadly, too-still grace.

"And then he'll partner me on my hunt," she

stated.

Relief coursed through Tanil, though short lived. The next second the strength in his legs gave out and he stumbled forward and hit the deck. On the edge of hurling up his guts, the cool tile and steel floor felt good against his cheek as his gag reflex kicked in.

His respect for Scharsi rose another notch. The woman was a genius and completely on target with her eight-minute warning, considering he'd felt fine the last couple of days clear up until this very moment. The meds she'd given him worked just as she'd said, though she hadn't quite explained what she'd meant by "sick as a dog" at the time she'd directed him to swallow the stuff. Well, the delayed action drug made him look every bit the sick man she'd just claimed him to be.

Along with a glob of bile, Tanil swallowed his relief that Scharsi had apparently taken him up on his offer to help her as he was hustled in one direction and she in another…just after he'd blown chunks on the Sealy asshole's shoes.

Yep, Scharsi was definitely a keeper.

* * * * *

With the towel draped around her neck, Scharsi wiped away the sweat that trailed down the exposed skin of her stomach. She wished she could just strip right here in the sparring room. Luckily her assigned quarters weren't far and a shower was just the ticket. She wondered how Tanil was doing. She hadn't seen him since he'd been hauled off to medical two days ago.

Before she knew it, her feet were headed away from her dorm room and toward the sick facility.

"Hold a minute, beautiful."

Scharsi halted in her tracks and turned slowly toward the voice. Sealy Garrison. Damn. Now this was a very pretty man. Though a bit rough around the edges, it appealed to her, yet he didn't stir the faintest flutter in her womb. Not like Tanil. Something about that bastard sent her life signs off the charts and engaged all her senses. Maybe it was her imagination? Perhaps she needed to get closer to the person standing in front of her, get a good whiff of him to drive the scent of Tanil out of her memory?

Just then, Mr. Pretty pushed away from the wall.

"Hey there, my big-legged beauty."

Okaay? He made her sound like an equine specimen. Scharsi had never actually seen one, but her neuro education, or rather

Amalgamation indoctrination, covered several courses in Earth and galactic history as far back as the archives went. It included wild and domesticated animals, like horses. She'd heard somewhere that horses were still found on Earth, but she'd never actually been to that side of the planet during her training days. Now that she thought about it, she hadn't been there in her commanding days either.

Her thoughts snapped back to her present company. The way he looked her up and down, she wondered if she should neigh now.

"Wanna try again, stud?" she queried, not bothering to school her features or keep her honey-blonde brows from arching in challenge.

"It's just that I love curvy hips and a luscious ass on a female. Especially a human. And your legs? Damn. All that sleek muscle perfectly packed on your thighs and calves makes my dick hard."

"Bet you say that to all the girls," she quipped, flattered he found her attractive, but no bells or whistles went off. She did blush, though.

"Darlin', there are very few females who look like you. Short 'n sassy, honey-blond curls, even paler eyes and all that coffee-and-cream skin. It's quite a contrast."

Short? She was damn near one point eighty-nine meters, no more than twelve or so centimeters shorter than himself.

With each word he'd stepped just a bit closer until they were practically nose to nose.

Hmm. He smelled good. A finely tuned man, honed for battle or a night of rough raunchy sex. It'd been awhile since she'd seen either, though she had to admit that Tanil's talented mouth had taken the edge off.

Sealy's lips lowered and captured hers in a coaxing kiss.

Should she push him away? She and Tanil weren't exclusive. They weren't even dating. They'd shared a few kisses and he'd given her the tongue lashing of her life, but she didn't own him and he didn't own her. Perhaps she could get her life back to normal by dating again? Puh. Again? Hell, to say she was doing something again meant she'd had to have done it before. Sigh. Gods, she was such a relationship virgin it was downright frustrating.

"Uh, you with me, Scharsi?" Sealy. Crap. She'd almost forgotten he was supposed to be kissing her. Her brain had been so hard and heavy into what was on her mind she'd tuned right out. Hmmp. Now that said a lot. One thing was certain, Tanil had no problem getting and keeping her attention.

"Well, damn. Can't say that's ever happened to me before."

"Huh? What?" she mumbled.

Sealy chuckled good-naturedly as his long fingers traipsed up and down her back. No shivers. No goose bumps. Nothin'.

"Can't say I've ever had a woman tune out on me before. First time for everything, eh?"

No need to play games with the man. Wasn't her style. "Guess so, Sealy. Hope you don't hold it against me. My mind is just somewhere else." The words were spoken quietly against his ear. He tightened his arms around her, dropped a kiss to her forehead and released her.

A thought cleared her head. Or was that a sound? Scharsi instructed her brain to turn down her audio filter and let the more subtle noises most humans miss flow into her. Keen hearing picked up the barest intake of breath, the increase in both breathing and heart rate and...a barely suppressed snarl?

Scharsi stepped away just as Sealy turned his head and gently bit down on her lip. He held on for a second, then released it slowly to rasp against his teeth. Raising her lashes to look past his shoulders, her gaze clashed with a pair of feline-like eyes that were becoming as familiar as her own — Tanil. Yet the inaudible rumbling in his chest was a complete surprise. The man was far from happy.

"Tanil?" she asked a bit warily. "I thought you were still in medical."

His eyes flashed in answer. Body rigid yet loose at the same time, his expression was as smooth and unruffled as heated synthsilk. But his heart rate and body temp were another story. The man was pissed.

But why? She had a clue, but it didn't make sense. They had no claims on one another. He was free to do as he pleased, just as Carl had been. And she was free to do as she pleased. Right? So why didn't it feel right?

"I'm as good as new. Can we talk?" His gaze pinned to Sealy's. "Privately."

"Let's finish this up later, shall we, darlin'?" the handsome Sealy asked as he stepped away slowly. The sparkle in his eyes said he knew good and well there would be no "later".

With a noncommittal shrug, Scharsi moved toward Tanil, her focus solely on him now.

"What do we need to talk about?"

The man took her by the crook of her elbow and attempted to haul her back to her quarters. Strangely enough, she was so intrigued by his behavior that she let him.

Tanil pressed his code into the digital keypad and the door slid open.

"How the hell does your key code work on my door?" Scharsi snapped, yanking her arm away.

Instead of an answer, Scharsi found herself backed against the wall just over the threshold. Quick as a whip, a titanium blade cleared its scabbard and pressed against the pulse of the man snarling in her face.

He didn't back up a hair.

"You may as well kill me, because I won't stop until I've wiped the taste of that bastard from your mouth."

Well, there was no way in hell she was lowering her knife considering such unusual possessiveness. He pressed forward in spite of the blade. A thin line of blood welled up around the metal, but Scharsi found herself kissed silly anyway.

Scharsi wondered if the gravity manager was malfunctioning. She was so far away from knowing up from down that she pushed away

from the devastating mouth and hands holding
her brain captive. She flipped her blade away
from Tanil's vulnerable throat and stared at him.
She couldn't think of a single thing to say. And
"wow" just didn't seem adequate.

But this wasn't supposed to happen.
Something about Tanil left her raw and achy,
and not inside her cunt, but inside her chest. Her
head. Her heart.

"I don't give a shit what's going on in that
beautiful head of yours, you're mine and will
remain mine. Didn't our talk aboard your ship
mean anything? Carl would want you happy.
And I want you, period. Keep that in mind the
next time some smooth talker comes sniffing
after your ass."

Even biting her lip, it still proved impossible
to suppress a grin at Tanil's grumbled, "Sealy.
Puh. I should sneak him some of that throw up
shit you gave me," followed by an even
grumblier, "guess I'll be back in medical for i-
stitches. Damn woman." And he was out the
door, headed back to the medical wing.

But the man had been right. She couldn't
remember the taste or feel of, uh, what's-his-
name?

The con beeped. A sexy-as-hell electronic

voice sounded into the room.

"Scharsi Knowles, report to the hub, please. Scharsi Knowles to the hub immediately for appointment with Ulric Vonner."

After two days at The Web being told Vonner was unexpectedly detained, the male would send for her now that she needed a cold shower. Sigh. Men.

Chapter Seven

Sealy arrived at her door just as she'd stepped out into the hall.

"Vonner sent me to get you."

After that, not a word was spoken as they moved quietly through the halls. Both of them bristled with weapons, but not even their boots made a sound. Sealy broke the silence.

"So, beautiful, care to share the details of how you've come to be here?"

"No."

"Okay, how about we fuck like rabid sex resort workers and I coax it out of you while you're sated?"

Scharsi's rich laughter burst right out of her chest. "You're a bold one. Skipped the hugs, kisses and all the touchy stuff and went straight for the fucking. Damn, Sealy, I had you pegged for the romantic type." She laughed harder, her voice laced with what she hoped sounded like good natured sarcasm.

They arrived at an unmarked door where Tanil waited. A much-too-familiar guilt tapped Scharsi on the shoulder. She hadn't meant to cut him. But certainly he must be okay if he was standing here, right?

Tanil must have caught the fact that she was a bit anxious. Scharsi could have kissed the man when he discreetly eased down the very front of his synthsilk tee, stretching the collar as if it were too tight, and it was just enough for her to see there was no blood, no cut. Hell, there wasn't even a scar. That must have been some super-duper i-stitch material the med staff used on him.

Sealy caught her attention, winked, placed his palm over the metal plate above the door lock and then stepped back to allow her to enter.

Scharsi strode inside without a single moment's hesitation. She had no idea what awaited on the other side, but it simply wasn't in her to do anything other than boldly face a challenge. Her feet didn't stop moving until she stood on the other side of a desk from the man she'd been waiting to see for days — Ulric Vonner, runner of all things BHI and badass extraordinaire, from what she'd heard.

She automatically stood at ease and waited patiently. Ulric Vonner studied her with cool confidence. Scharsi studied him right back. Finally he spoke as he held out a pouch to her. A quick peek revealed identification and passage papers.

"I took the liberty of giving you a last name. I assumed it wouldn't bother you since word has it, Commander…"

"It's just Scharsi."

"Right. Well, Scharsi, word has it that you're dead." Vonner's gaze swung to Tanil. "You, however, are questionable."

The expression etched across Vonner's face said he knew more about her and her new "friend" than he let on. Scharsi wasn't surprised. It was this man's job to know who was coming and going at The Web. But just how much did he know? The word "everything" popped into her head as she studied him with unwavering eyes.

"Well, as you can see, I'm far from dead, but I'd like to keep that knowledge from going any further than this facility. As for Tanil, only he can tell you his story. Does this change our plans?" Scharsi asked matter-of-factly.

Vonner flashed her a smile so wicked Scharsi wasn't sure whether to be thrilled or reach for her guns.

"The request for a bounty mission to hunt down and capture the murderer of one Dr. Carl Sabbo has been received and paid in full. The assignment is yours."

Tanil's expression read confused, but Scharsi wasn't about to enlighten him of the fact that she was the one who'd put up the bounty on Carl's murderer. Besides, there were no rules that said the person who placed the bounty couldn't be the one who hunted the prey.

"So, about that last name?" Vonner asked with more snark in his voice than Scharsi cared for.

"I'll pass on that, sir. Thanks."

He held his hand out for the doc pouch. "No problem. I'll have these reworked and ready for your departure."

"And when are we cleared to leave?" Scharsi asked, wondering if there were any other surprises.

"So, I assume Captain Tanil is your partner in this endeavor?"

"Yes sir."

"In that case, you can leave whenever you want. In fact, the sooner the better. Not necessarily for us, but for him."

"Meaning?"

Vonner blew her off. And if there was anything Scharsi hated, it was being blown off. But forcing this man's hand, and she could definitely force his hand, wasn't in her best interest so she let is slide.

"You'll find a full issue of BHI gear in your dorm unit. Anything else you need, just let me, Con or Sealy know. Be advised that we took a few liberties with your ship."

"What exactly to you mean by liberties, Mr. Vonner?" Scharsi's expression was stone hard and the only thing that gave away her annoyance was the deep timbre in her throat.

"Hold a second. And that's just plain Vonner to you, young lady. None of that mister stuff. Understood?" Without waiting for her answer, he gave a quick tap on the unit on the conference room table. A vid screen embedded into one wall of the room flared to life.

"Dex here."

"Dex," Vonner said, "this is a new hunter, Scharsi, and her partner. You've done some work on her ship. Give the woman an update."

An appreciative whistle preceded Dex's words.

"First of all, Scharsi, my compliments on your ship. The Futsuka-shi is one fine piece of work. If I'm not mistaken, regardless of her downplayed paint job, she's a war class cruiser with military grade components and upgrades.

Bigger, faster and definitely more equipped than most. Even her medical facilities are impressive, as if she were a med cruiser before or something."

Scharsi didn't respond.

"Get on with it, Dex. Kissing her ass won't tell her what she needs to know," Vonner said.

Dex rolled his eyes, then ignored Ulric. His gaze remained on Scharsi as he explained what he'd done to her ship.

"The jump drive needed some tweaking. She was in okay shape, but probably felt a little squirrely the last time you used it. We upgraded it so it should really fly good and stable. A few of your crystolium cells were low so we topped you up and restocked some of your supplies, everything from spare repair parts to replicator materials and food. Anything you need that's not already aboard can be picked up at any supply port. Direct communication with The Web across secure channels was programmed into your central computer as well as a new con system. The old one was pretty good, but in order to use our stealth frequencies I had to directly program them. You'll find coordinating comm tabs in your gear in the dorms. To use it, just press it behind your ear. Tap it when you need to call the computer on your ship or to reach us here."

"What about communicating with each other?" Tanil asked.

"Yep, they'll do that too."

Scharsi almost shuddered. She already had unwanted equipment embedded behind her left ear. Now she'd have to stick something behind her right?

"Can these comm tabs be traced? Set to self-destruct?"

"They can only be traced by us. We use a bit of a different kind of tracking that's pretty much unhackable by anyone else. As for self-destruct, yes. That's totally within your control," Dex said calmly as if he did this every day. Hell, she guessed he did do this everyday.

"We made sure not to touch your med-tech and left your sickbay room intact. But we did have to make a structural change to your spare crew quarters. It's been converted into a holding cell."

Sigh.

Which meant Tanil would have to either bunk with her, climb back into the med-tech or sleep in the head. The thought of the first option sent a blush up her neck. Times like this, Scharsi wished she were a Generation Eleven. At least then she'd see everything from a logical point of view rather than a biological one, plus have the ability to control blood flow to certain parts of her body…including the one flaming so hotly right now in her pants.

Dex looked down at a touchpad in his hands, checked off a few items, then said, "I think that about does it."

"Thanks, Dex. Out," Vonner said. Another quick tap and the vid screen went gray and faded to nothing more than another piece of wall.

Scharsi took a deep breath, relaxed and let her brain process all the changes Dex had just rattled off to her. Making a mental note to check each one personally, she put one last request to Mr. Mystery Bounty and Stuff, Inc., the head hunter himself.

"Vonner, I'd like to take a couple of days and make use of your halo training room, rest up a little bit."

"It'll be our pleasure to have you around another day or so. I can schedule a personal tour if you like. Sealy?"

The man had stepped quietly back into the room and stood leaning lazily against a wall toward the back.

"You're one of us now. You'll have whatever you need. Even if it's to kick Sealy's ass for being such a damn pussy hunter. Welcome to BHI, Scharsi." Vonner chuckled and extended his hand with a grin. "Oh, and as for the reason the Amalgamation won't claim the good captain here is one of theirs, all I'll say is that the coordinates to the contacts you'll need to help you are already programmed into your navigation system. Get to them. Fast."

Scharsi resisted the urge to tilt her head in question and narrow her eyes at the man. Instead she took the offered hand. Hell, she even managed to chuckle. Couldn't help it at Tanil's exasperated sigh when Vonner turned, nodded to him and said, "Oh, and welcome to you too, Tannie."

Then both Vonner and Sealy exited without another word.

* * * * *

After that little introduction to Vonner this morning, Tanil hadn't been able to get one minute of Scharsi's time. It had been one meeting after another for both of them. First there was training on all the gear assigned to them as BHI hunters. Most of it appeared standard issue, but almost every piece had something different in the design, some kind of subtle hard-to-spot modification. Genius, really. In short, BHI was no punk outfit. They had the best of everything and no expense was spared. Too bad the Amalgamation was on his shit list. They would have loved to get their hands on some of this stuff.

After weapons and gear training, Tanil had been hauled back to medical for a check up while Scharsi went to work out. Gods, how he'd wanted to see that. It was a sight he had yet to behold as he'd never come upon her practicing with her blades while aboard her ship. Too bad. Just the thought of a glimpse of the woman in action sent his blood on a one way trip south.

Next, instructions on everything from accessing credits and using their new identities, to protocol for accepting future jobs or simply taking time off. It was like military boot camp all over again, only without getting kicked in the ribs for pissing off the artillery instructor.

Finally his quaking muscles and loudly protesting empty belly forced him into the cafeteria for a bite. Scharsi hadn't been there. However, he had met two of the coolest humanoids. First, there was Aurelie, one of the cooks for The Web. She'd made sure Tanil had a meal he recognized and enjoyed. With all the various species in Amalgamation space, not to mention the number of races in this quadrant alone, Tanil had been a bit concerned for his palate after he'd walked in and caught of whiff of what smelled like fermented tuckmanoe long past its days of swimming in the open Merovian Seas. While Aurelie had coaxed him into actually sampling the food, her expressive and unusually violet eyes held a bit of sparkle as she entertained him with tales of her childhood growing up on Aboo.

Particularly interesting were the holiday trips to see her grandparents at the communes on Qxri. Apparently that old couple, her mother's parents, were still quite cough active in their communities as sexual aid specialists. In between stories that had him almost choking on his dinner with laughter, the slender spitfire kept the other hunters in line with an occasional snap of a wet towel when they didn't bus their own dishes to the rotating conveyor that carried everything to the back for sanitizing. Even with the occasional yelp-inducing towel snap, Aurelie had still been a sweetheart about it.

Still laughing about sex resort stories, Tanil

paused mid-hack when a breathtaking female with the most unusual features came into the cafeteria. What a piece of work this one was. Not just because of the fall of white-blond hair swinging clear down to her waist, nor the overlarge eyes just a shade lighter than Aurelie's purplish hues. But because she walked into the cafeteria with an energy that belied her small frame. It was as if the woman had been shot out of a gun! Then there was no doubt this one was trouble with a capital "T" when she'd had the nerve to walk right up to him and say, "So, how's the Qxri beef-n-zava, Tanil? Not exactly what they'd feed you at your mama's house, but it'll do, eh?" Uncanny that she knew his name, but he'd chalked it up to being the new kid on the block and figured Vonner or that asshat Sealy had told her about him.

But when she said, "So, you're all hot, bothered and horny? Bet it ain't the beef Aurelie fed you. Stop fretting. She'll be there when you get back to your room."

His fork paused halfway between his mouth and his plate. Was she a psychic or something?

"I'm not a psychic, but I am pretty good about picking feelings out of the air. Oh, I'm Zeri, by the way."

An empath? Fuck. Judging by the way she'd snatched his emotions out of the nether while he'd been laughing with Aurelie to cover up his ache for Scharsi, this Zeri was a damn strong reader.

With a wicked grin, saucy dip of her hip and wink at a departing and grinning Aurelia, Zeri headed back to the kitchen to wreak havoc, no doubt. She was a bona fide troublemaker minus the attitude, and Tanil liked her immediately.

Finally done with his meal, Zeri appeared and cleared his plate just as he rose to leave the common room. "Since you're new I'll cut you a break and take care of these for you. Next time through, don't forget to clear your own dishes. Oh, and a little something to take care of that, uh, longing. And no, it's not for you."

A little package was pressed into his hand as Zeri shooed him toward the door. Tanil took the little opaque plastic container without comment, too physically wiped out to argue or bother with questions.

Striding down the hall, his pace kicked up all on its own. Bedtime. The thought brought a fiercely intense ache for the one woman he had barely seen all day. Scharsi. He needed her. Needed to be near her, to hold her. To lie next to her and inhale the clean natural scent of her hair. To play with the neat little bundles and twists that she wore it in. And, if she would have him, to ease into her hot, dewy channel. To bask in the warmth of her sex. To ride her into oblivion until they both fell into a deep coma-like sleep.

Plain and simple, he missed her. All of her.

Exhausted, but determined, Tanil headed straight to their room. Once inside he immediately sought out Scharsi. He'd been as surprised as she'd been earlier when he'd returned from medical for the first time to discover they'd been assigned the same quarters. There were two small bedrooms in the dorm room, but he had no intention of laying anything down in the empty spare room except his gear bag.

"Eww, man. Take care of that," he grumbled at himself after getting a whiff of his own body odor. Yep, definitely a long day.

After a quick shower in the surprisingly large head, Tanil halfway dried off and headed toward Scharsi's room.

Not even bothering to be quiet or subtle, Tanil practically charged the bed. His ears weren't sensitive enough to pick up the almost inaudible whirr of the heating laser in the silence of the room, but he was no fool and expected the faint jolt of energy just below the skin that was common when in close proximity to a charging cell. Yep, she aimed for his lower ribs just as he pressed against her back.

Gods, he must be nuts. Engaging a sleeping Gen8? And not for the purpose of crossing her off the Amalgamation's CoK, Capture or Kill, list? Crazy was the only word for it. But he had to have her. As the day had worn on, he'd realized that not spending time with this woman wasn't even an option anymore.

He felt her turn slightly. Just enough light filtered down from the dimmed overhead unit — it never actually turned all the way off — for him to know that her eyes were on him.

"Tanil, what exactly do you think you're doing?" Scharsi's sleep-filled voice carried a hint of yawn mixed with curiosity.

"If I have to explain it, then I've really got to brush up on my technique."

The woman's answering smile devastated even in the dimly lit cabin. This wasn't the smile of an emotionless combination of genes and nanites. This was a warm, feminine, living, loving being. She might be able to pick him up with one arm and toss him across the room, but that didn't mean she didn't deserve to be loved. Deserve to be happy. Deserve to be his.

That damn laser was still aimed at his gut, but he pressed closer. If the skilled holo-doc could heal up the cut across his throat earlier, what would be a little hole in the chest from a laser pistol, right? Correction, another hole in the chest from a laser pistol.

There was no way Tanil would allow himself to be parted from Scharsi, not after the glorious night they'd spent exploring each other's bodies, minds, needs and emotions on her ship. And certainly not after the kiss he'd taken from her this morning. The animalistic flare of possession he'd experienced when he'd seen that Sealy playboy pressed up against Scharsi's lush body in the hallway earlier flew to the forefront of his mind. Damn poacher.

He eased his arm underneath her head so his biceps took the place of her pillow. And she allowed it, allowed him to wrap her up in the cocoon of his body, let him gently massage her slowly relaxing muscles with his free hand. Her fingers sank into the forearm on which her head rested as he worked his way from her wide, lovely hips, over the rigid ripple of her abs and up to the underside of a full, ripe breast. Tanil was rewarded with the thunk of her pistol hitting the dense rubberized floor. Seconds later came the rustle of sheets and blankets joining the weapon in an unkempt pile.

Trained to remain quiet under the worst of circumstances, Scharsi's single swift intake was more than he'd hoped for, though barely audible. The woman's breathing remained slow and even. It hadn't sped up at all, but deepened as her heart thumped like a drum against her ribs. Gods, he wanted to be the one to blow her control, make her writhe against him, beg him to slide into her body. Huh. Scharsi, beg? Imagining such a thing must truly be related to the male ego. He almost shook his head at himself. Instead he spoke to the sensuous creature lying with her back pressed flush against his swelling front.

The moment was perfect, like everything else about this woman.

"Do you like that, Scharsi? Tell me it feels good, beautiful."

She didn't answer, just sort of whimpered a bit and took another deep breath in. Tanil tugged a ripe berry-firm nipple between thumb and forefinger. The result — the slightest squirm of lush backside against his cock. Most men would have steered clear of her after a single glance at the honed machine that was her body. But underneath the sculpted mask of her face was not the cold calculated killer she'd been created to be. This was no ice queen. Scharsi's body temperature soared as he explored the terrain. Felt her jaw flex against the crook of his elbow as she clenched her teeth against the sensation of raw pleasure.

"Gods, woman, you feel so good against me." It was little more than a breath laced with words but it was all Tanil could manage.

"I'm not supposed to feel like this. I don't know what to do with it all," she whispered back, her breath warm and moist as she planted an open-mouthed kiss to his forearm.

Tanil nipped her neck muscle. It twitched under his tongue. The harder he sucked on that obviously sensitive spot, the more her breathing deepened until it finally became a soft, surprised-sounding moan.

He squeezed, kneaded and caressed every centimeter of flesh that could be reached from this position, everything from breast down to firm thigh. Tanil didn't have to be concerned with hurting her. This was no spun glass female. Scharsi was all woman. Even if she hadn't had the modified genes that gave her a buffed physique, she'd still have solid wide hips, a nice round ass and plenty to hold onto.

As he explored, Scharsi's own hands eased up to caress her breasts the way she liked. Tanil's fingers slid around and over the soft flesh at the crease of her pelvis. Slowly they danced over the close cropped curls at the vee of her body. While he worked the front of her, his hips instinctively ground his erection against her lovely backside.

With an easy tap on her inner thighs, she spread them invitingly. Without hesitation his fingers sought the prize hidden there, a slick and dewy treasure. Her sex was wet and swollen with need, barely hiding the bundle of nerves that he zeroed in on without err. The slightest pressure made her back arch and bow. He knew from experience that her lips were parting now while the inside of her bottom lip was taking a gentle punishment from her teeth.

This time he teased the sensitive flesh just above the hood of her clit, then eased around and along her labials, learning the pressure she liked, absorbing her reaction to each touch. Scharsi instinctively opened wider for him and her sex bloomed beneath his questing fingers.

"Yes. Touch me. Harder."

Instead of giving her what she asked for, he raised his fingers and inhaled her scent. Scharsi went still when Tanil groaned in appreciation. Sweet. Addictive. Damn.

Giving himself room to maneuver, Tanil planted a hand underneath Scharsi's hip, raised it from the bed and flipped her over on her stomach.

The light scrape of his nails gave him exactly what he wanted-the view of a beautifully curved spine and an ass meant for spanking that moved side to side, seeking, like a cat stretching beneath the morning suns. With her forehead pressed into what was left of the bedding Scharsi looked like a woman ready for a good long night of fucking.

"Ass up, head down, Scharsi."

* * * * *

And without hesitation, she obeyed. It had been a long time since she'd been on the receiving end of orders, in bed or otherwise. Tanil was naturally dominant. It had nothing to do with what she was. No egotistical need to rule over her just to prove he could top a SS. Every time he told her to roll over for him or to give up her orgasm, the woman Scharsi had kept locked away for most of her life wanted to submit. Compliance seemed natural, normal. Huh. Those were two words she'd never expected to associate with a love life.

Well, 'bout damn time.

"Shar? Where did you go just now?"

What? Scharsi went still, then wished she hadn't. She'd just told on herself without saying a single word. Just from what little she'd experienced of his skills in bed, Tanil would work overtime to make sure she was satisfied, even if it took him all night long. Damn, the man had some serious stamina. And SS or not, Scharsi held back a grin when her mind began to place silent bets with herself as to whether her pussy could take it or not.

"If you can zone out like that, woman, I'm not doing my job."

Fuck. Now she was in for it.

There was no way she was going to tell him what she'd really been thinking. The man knew he was talented in the sack and his head was as big as his cock already. Conceited ass. A rightfully conceited ass, but that wasn't the point.

"I was just thinking of how wonderful it is to have a lover. A talented lover who seems to like me as a person rather than seeing me as some oddity." Oh Gods, would he buy it? After all, it was pretty close to the truth.

"Uh huh."

Guess not.

Scharsi found herself pulled to the edge of the bed. A shift of the mattress was all the warning she got before Tanil was on his knees on the floor and diving for her pussy. It felts soooo good to have his mouth there, licking her slick folds, sucking her clit with just the right pressure—enough to make her squirm, but not enough to push her into orgasm.

Damn man.

The tip of his tongue pushed against her opening, fought with the tight ring of muscle guarding the entrance to her sex. Push, retreat, push, retreat. Lick, slide, suck. Gods, yes.

A long finger eased inside, giving her just a bit more friction, just enough to make the slick muscles of her pussy flex as they tried to keep him inside, to hold onto the lovely sensation as that long digit moved in, out, in, out.

Oh Gods, more. She was so close. In mere moments he had her on the verge.

"Please, more. Just a little."

"Not yet. I want you crazy for it first."

Well, that wouldn't take long. She spread her legs wider, balanced on one shoulder and added her own hand to the mix.

"Ow!"

Tanil bit her finger! Not hard, but enough to warn her that she was encroaching on his territory.

"Gods, you taste so fucking good. I don't want to share, not even with your fingers."

"Selfish…oh, yes. Bastard. Give it to me."

This time he bit the flesh just to the side, a tender spot on her inner thigh close to her labia. Teeth, lips and tongue — sharp and mellow, distinct and lazy.

Her breasts weren't overly large, but like all the rest of her engineered physique, they were proportioned with perfectly distributed nerves and blood vessels, and as a result, quite sensitive. So when he reached underneath to tease and twist her nipples, his manipulations were aided by the weight of her breasts from this angle. Each tormenting tug traveled up from her nipple and radiated through each sensitive globe.

And now it was time for him to fuck her. Gods, it just had to be time. If not, she'd disintegrate into nothing, like flesh hit by laser fire. When Scharsi's thighs began to tremble from the sensations he wrung from her body, she was ready to beg, and without shame.

Just as she opened her mouth to plead with Tanil, in one smooth move he was up on his feet, parted her folds with gentle fingers and slid deep with anything but gentleness. Hard. Fast. Endless. Just how she liked it.

She was sure every nerve fired between her sex and her brain and back again faster than traveling through a wormhole, faster than the speed of light. And she met him stroke for stroke, craving, needing him so deep inside that there was no distinguishing the one from the other.

He slammed in. Her hips shifted. They met in the middle and it was explosive, bright and beautiful, yet knife-edged, dark, stormy. Then he retreated to that teasing stroke he loved to stoke her fires with—nothing more than the head of his cock tripping over the tight ring of muscle just inside her channel.

Deep again.

Pulled back.

Then deeper still until her head spun wildly.

"Can I come? Please, can I, can I, can I?" she babbled, unable to help herself. Only Tanil made her lose it, stripped her of the control that had been stomped into her from an early age. Only this man had the ability to take her down to her most base emotions, made her reach for them rather than recoil back into analytics and reasoning. Only him.

And it scared the shit out of her…but only until he increased his speed and opened his mouth.

"There's nothing in the 'verse like this. Like being inside of you, joining my soul with yours. Fucking amazing."

Wow.

"I could fuck you all day and night. I swear I wish we didn't have somebody to go kill. That's it. Take it, baby. Take all of me."

And then he was home, sliding his thick cock into her soaked flesh until he was seated. And once he was all the way in, he pushed just the tiniest bit more.

One hand held fast to her hip, the other found its way to her clit. Six quick strokes and she was done. It was over. Her world exploded behind her eyes. Somewhere off in the distance she heard Tanil call her name as the muscled walls of her dewy pussy contracted around him so strongly she felt it from her womb clear down to the tightly flexed muscles of her Achilles tendon.

Yes, he curled her toes.

Tanil settled across her back. She welcomed the weight, welcomed it grounding her, settling her once again.

Just as Scharsi drifted off, she was startled awake by her man's mumbled, "Crap, I almost forgot," followed by a rush from the bed into the small common area that joined their bedrooms. He returned with a small plastic-looking box.

"Zeri sent this. She's one of the cooks here. I figure you two have met since she sent this for you."

"Me? Why would she send this for me? I haven't been to the cafeteria at all today. Didn't get to meet any staff at all."

"You haven't eaten all day, Scharsi?"

Tanil's tone was a bit heated with more censure than anyone had ever used with her, other than her former trainers or Carl when he felt she was doing something stupid.

Hmm. This time when thoughts of Carl pushed into her head, they didn't bring a wash of guilt and pain. Instead she experienced a gratitude that warmed her heart. Gratitude and thankfulness that she'd had a friend like him. A

friend who'd taught her that she was worthy of
life and love. Worthy to be more than a tool.
And now she had another friend. Correction—
friend and lover—who was just as solid of
character as Carl had been. Even when he was
fussing at her.

"Scharsi, you know your body needs almost
three times the protein as the typical humanoid
to keep your muscles healthy. What's with this
skipping meals bullshit?"

"I didn't mean to. I just ran out of time."
And she couldn't believe she was explaining this
to Tanil. But for some reason she felt a deep
desire to please him rather than tell him to kiss
her ass since she could take care of herself.

He cast her a sidelong glance complete with
a fierce frown, curled lip and an expression full
of "yeah, right" as he popped open the top of the
container.

Instantly the element in the bottom of the
box heated and the scent of some kind of meat
and sweet veggie wafted into the space between
Scharsi and Tanil.

"Wow. Whoever this Zeri is, remind me to
thank her, will you?" Scharsi said with real
surprise. She sat up, accepting the container
from Tanil, who'd produced a little eating

utensil from a compartment on the side of the box.

When she was done, Tanil took the lid off the second box.

"Lillee pudding! How did she know?" At Tanil's shrug, Scharsi was almost at a loss for words. As she navigated that first bite, which she knew would be heavenly, she said, "Yep, this Zeri is my new best friend…well, after you of course."

Chapter Eight

Vulf Destry paced in front of the wall of men at attention in front of his desk. The room was as silent as the blackness of space itself. The rubberized soles of his boots made no sound on the hard tiled floor as short, almost choppy steps moved him back and forth. His gaze drilled through his visitors. Both the men and the Super Soldiers kept their focus on the holoportrait of the IMF leadership displayed behind him. None dared look him in the eye.

"Irritated" didn't begin to describe his state of mind and murderous didn't come close to his current inclination. Fingers itched to pull the sidearm from the holster at his waist and simply end this entire debacle. Two things kept him from doing so—one, he would never make it out of this room alive if he tried, and two, he needed answers to what the hell had gone wrong.

Straightening his already perfect dark gray uniform, Vulf came to a halt. He couldn't reveal his anger, not now. The team must believe that he still trusted them, still believed in them. Otherwise, reassigning the humans and exterminating the Super Soldiers could get messy. When he was sure red-hot anger would not resonate in his words, he finally spoke.

"This entire team was present at the assignment regarding the fugitive criminal, Dr. Carl Sabbo, yes?"

As a single voice, all six answered, "Yes sir."

"And the mission was successful, yes?"

Again, "Yes sir."

"And what of the secondary assignment?"

For a moment, Vulf thought no one would give the obvious answer considering they'd all been briefed on the unexpected circumstances that made this little meeting necessary in the first place.

Finally, KE-0V217 stepped forward. Good. This was all his fault anyway.

"When the fugitive was apprehended, he made a sudden move. Being unfamiliar with the layout of the dwelling and not knowing whether armed accomplices were present, we defended ourselves. The fugitive was killed. Captain Tanil was caught in the crossfire just as intelligence came through the con that the Captain was wanted for questioning in regard to an internal investigation."

Vulf dismissed the humans. At the quiet

snap of the door closing, he captured the gaze of
the remaining things in the room as he paced
again. Both would have been aware of the kill
order for Dr. Sabbo given to the Gen10 and the
kill order for Captain Taikiji given to KE-0V217,
but neither would ever say a word. After all,
conversations between Amalgamation personnel
or property that was overheard via auditory
filter was considered eavesdropping. Special
rules had been created for just such a situation
that included all kinds of fun punishments for
those that used their embedded equipment to
spy on others. It didn't matter that the rules only
applied to Super Soldiers. They weren't people
after all, only property, pieces of machinery,
slabs of meat with intelligence built in. Nothing
more. But it didn't change the fact they could
hear the quietest footfall up to five hundred
meters away.

"So then, you fired the accidental shot that
downed the good captain, correct?"

"I did as I was ordered." Basically this SS
was saying absolutely nothing in front of his
fellow soldier to implicate himself in the Tanil
situation. But Vulf's patience was running out as
the moments ticked by without a true answer to
what the hell had happened, or rather not

happened.

"Fine." He turned to the Super Soldier on his left. "Engage your auditory filter at max." A few seconds ticked by. "KE-0V217, you will tell me whether you carried out your orders. Now."

"Yes sir. It was a rather simple assignment, especially for me."

The sneer on the SS's face made it clear what he thought of all of this. Probably what he thought of every man who wasn't his superior kind — a genetic fleshbag of perfected DNA. Fucking Super Soldier. No, worse, Gen8 Gamma Project. It was bad enough the IMF had created the perfect enhanced walking, talking weapon, but then they'd gone and made them brainiacs as well, slaves to logic and reason alone. But that wasn't the worst fuck up. Oh no, not even close. The worst fuck up in all of history was the fact the IMF purposely falsified the records to show that they'd all been terminated, when in fact quite a few had been kept around to carry out "special assignments" such as this one. Then along came fuckup to the second power — claiming the stock was destroyed meant deactivating the tags that guaranteed a blip on the radar if they ever went AWOL. After all, how in the hell could they explain Super Soldier locations and data popping up in the asset database if the SS associated with the serial numbers were supposed to be history? The bastards were tough to track and even harder to find. All that meant to Vulf was that tighter leashes were needed. And tightening collars around necks was his specialty.

He stared into the uncanny eyes of these hulking animals and wondered at the mental capacity of his superiors. Their decisions were typically stupid, stupid and more stupid. But now it was time to cut to the chase.

"You checked the body, made sure he wasn't breathing?"

"There was no need. He is simply human, nothing special. Never mind the crater left in his chest. There is no way former Captain Tanil Taikiji survived the wound."

"You're sure?" Vulf challenged.

"Of course. I am never wrong and I never miss. Check the stats in my file. The results of every neuro-education evaluation show that I am ninety-eight point six percent accurate in the execution of any plan."

"Well, my friend, you missed the mark. I'll make sure your record is modified to reflect your new ninety-seven percent accuracy rating.

"Excuse me?" The hulking SS with lightning bolts tattooed on his scalp, the body of an all-endurance machine and the face of bland stewed zava drew down his brows and took a menacing step forward. Time to end this. Vulf might hold a higher spot on the food chain than the two humanoids in this room, but he wasn't so self-assured as to be an idiot. His present company were elite fighters trained to do nothing but kill. And did he mention there were two of them?

"I said, you idiot, you missed." And that was all Vulf had to say. He turned and stalked from the room, leaving the Super Soldiers standing there. Let their dumb-assed handlers come and fetch them, or they could stand there until the worlds ended for all he cared.

Sigh.

It was times like this he wished the unnatural bastards worked alone rather than in units. It would be easier to pull off his next move.

* * * * *

Kev took his time leaving Destry's office, though from the line of questioning he'd just endured he didn't have much time. If he was going to get Commander Scharsi and Captain Taikiji to their next meeting he would have to work fast. His superiors were already aware of this little interrogation by Vulf. He typically detested allowing them to listen in on his conversations, but logic dictated that those manipulating the puppet strings behind the scenes be aware of little episodes like this.

He'd expected nothing different. In fact, Kev was surprised it had taken Vulf this long to figure out what had really happened that day on Ukure. Slow, these humans.

He looked down at his watch, did a few mental calculations and said quietly, "It's done, as you heard. Give me ten days."

Kev then tapped the transmitter carefully hidden by his hair just above the hairline at the base of his skull.

A click and a beep told him he'd disconnected.

Yes, he had to move fast. If Vulf knew that Tanil was alive, then it was only a matter of time before his own records were uncovered. He must have all the pieces in place before that happened. If word got out that his records were manipulated to show he was a Gen10 SS instead of a Gen8 Gamma, not only would he be terminated before he could complete his mission, but a whole lot of operatives with similar circumstances would be outed.

Fuck. Ten days. His calculations had better be correct or they were all royally screwed.

* * * * *

After three hard weeks of training, which she put on herself, and equally hard loving, which Tanil put on her, Scharsi was more than ready to get on with the hunt. Only now, the knowledge that she didn't have to go it alone both comforted and terrified her. A more worthy lover and partner Scharsi couldn't have hoped for. Though she was the engineered party in the relationship, Tanil seemed to have been created just for her. His temperament balanced hers out. His natural patience and caring shored up her tattered emotions and helped heal old wounds she'd thought long resolved. She could see herself working, playing, living and loving such a man from now until whenever. Yet knowing that he walked around in plain 'ole human skin was enough to scare the living hell out of her.

He had no enhanced senses. No super speed or hearing. He didn't even have the benefit of her tougher skin. And worse, while they walked into the middle of a potential biological hazard, Tanil had no bioengineered resistance to disease. With all these things against him, he'd still refused to stay behind. In fact he'd pretty much melted away her resolve with the torch of his anger when he realized she actually wanted to leave him at The Web.

His hurt had been palpable when he'd thought she didn't believe in him, didn't think he had it in him to "handle the mission" as he put it. Of course that hadn't been what she'd meant at all. She'd only wanted him to be safe, but Scharsi couldn't blame him for his feelings. After all, if he'd suggested she remain behind she would have felt the same.

A crooked smile lay across her lips at the thought of the making up she'd had to do last night. It had taken quite a bit of work on her part to get him back in a decent mood. Her pussy clenched at the remembered sensation of having him fill her. Scharsi felt herself turning on and up, regardless of the fact that her pussy was a bit sore. Amazing how even with her advanced genetics Tanil still managed to work her over. Mmm mmm mmm.

After a final briefing with Vonner early this morning, they were packed and aboard her ship in record time. She had no idea where they were going, only that Vonner was sending her to meet a contact who could get her close to the men she'd identified as Carl's successful and Tanil's attempted murderers. Wherever it was remained top secret, period. So instead of learning the location, she'd agreed to allow someone, she had no idea who, to program her ship's computer to automatically enter autopilot once they cleared the Smith Gate and emerged wherever they were supposed to end up.

A small army of Dex's assistants swarmed over her ship, making last-minute adjustments and double-checking to ensure everything worked correctly. The second they cleared out of her personal space, Scharsi practically bolted to the bridge to begin the sequence that would get them the hell out of there. People. Way too many people. Even though none of them looked at her with judgmental eyes or accusatory stares, she wasn't sure she'd ever be used to having so many "normal" guys underfoot.

So where was Tanil? Hmmm. She hadn't seen him since she boarded two hours ago. Keeping an eye on Dex's crew and running from one end of the ship to another to plug in this, or check on that, had been a full-time job. In fact, Scharsi hadn't had a moment to check her quarters to see if their gear bags were on board, let alone locate Tanil in the flesh. Yet in the silence of the bridge, looking at the star charts and thinking on the vastness of the black where there was nothing but space and more space, Scharsi's insides clenched with yearning. She needed Tanil's presence, needed his warmth, his "realness". The knowledge that she'd gone so many years without something as simple as being with him without realizing how much she needed this kind of connection rocked her back on her heels.

Moments later, the skin on the back of Scharsi's neck tingled and danced, but not with alarm or wariness. He was near, the man she'd so quickly become addicted to. He hadn't said a word since entering the bridge, hadn't touched her either, yet she felt him clear down to the undercurve of her ass. She surprised herself when she disengaged her auditory filter without a thought, all so she could listen to him move up behind her. Another fifteen centimeters and he'd be close enough to kiss her on the neck just below her right ear in that spot she liked so much. It crossed her mind to admit that little fact was the reason she wore her hair up more and more these days.

Nah.

Pushing away the mushiness of the moment,

Scharsi strapped herself into her seat. The very creases of her palms itched. One hand wanted to engage the console to get a peek at the coordinates keyed into her navigation system, the other wanted to play in the silky mass of hair on Tanil's head.

Instead she hit the con and said, "This is the Futsuka-shi, ID S24, prepared for departure."

"This is the Web space dock. Copy that, S24. Please remain in your bay. You are ninth in the queue."

"Hunting must be busy work if I have to wait that long to get out of here. Cut a woman a break, will you, Dex?" She enjoyed picking at Dex. He had such an awesome sense of humor. Not to mention he was one of the best damn computronics specialists she'd ever met. In fact she couldn't think of a single SS trained in AI and comp-analytics who could hold a flash to Dex.

"The answer I'd give to any other woman would be to stop whining and wait your turn, but since you're such a beautiful female who humors me and doesn't try to kick my ass, I'll see what I can do. Oh, and tell Tannie that I promise I'm not trying to poach like Sealy is."

Tanil dropped into the co-captain's chair

next to her and burst out laughing. He leaned forward, leading with that stubborn chin of his, and hit a sequence of buttons on the console.

"Dex, this is Tannie. Gods, I hate that name, but thanks so much for the reassurance."

"Anytime, man. Anytime. Hold a moment."

Dex dropped off and Scharsi allowed herself to enjoy the moment, chuckling quietly and shaking her head in disbelief at the men's banter. It all felt so wonderfully…normal. She looked up and snapped her mouth shut.

Tanil eyed her with an intensity that sucked all the air from her lungs. The humor that had danced in his eyes a second before had been replaced with flat-out lust. Need was clearly written on his face, in the way his lips pressed together, the gleam in his eye as he watched from the side with his head tilted at a certain angle, the way his lips parted and the tip of his tongue slowly eased across his front teeth. He wanted her and made no secret about it.

In a semi-stupor, Scharsi watched him rise from his chair. It was almost as if he uncurled his powerful frame one taut muscle at a time and each movement melted her muscles to the point where she simply couldn't move — not even when he turned her chair away from the con, trapped her knees between his and braced his hands on the armrests of her chair.

Tanil bent at the waist and took her mouth with his own.

Scharsi was unable to control the reaction to his nearness. Automatically she opened her mouth and breathed in, drew the scent of the man into her lungs.

When she thought to take over the kiss, Tanil devoured, ravished, took relentlessly, and yet gave so much more. His fingers left the nape of her neck and trailed down the side of her throat to tease her collarbone through the synthsilk of her new BHI uniform. Her breasts swelled, thrummed as they strained upward, wanting him to hurry and touch her there.

He broke the kiss and said, "Ninth in the queue means we could be sitting here for at least an hour and a half, beautiful."

She pressed kisses to both sides of his mouth between words. "Yes." A lick at his bottom lip had him opening to her again. "Could be an hour. Maybe more."

"So, how should we spend the time, Scharsi?" Gods, she loved the way he said her name. Her uniform was too hot. Her fingers pinched the tab to slide the zipper down. Naked.

She needed to be naked.

Beep. beep. beep.

Damn it. The con sounded again.

"Ignore it," Tanil suggested. She would have, but all systems were prepped for takeoff, which meant the ship's AI automatically received and relayed any and all messages from space dock for both the Smith Gate and The Web.

"Futsuka-shi, this is the dockmaster. Please proceed from your bay to dock six. You are now second in the queue. Departure in six minutes for arrival at the Gate in fifteen minutes. You are pre-cleared for FTL through the Smith, so no waiting unless you count the time it takes your computer to upload the entry sequence, perform diagnostics and download back to the Gate crew just prior to entry."

"Fuck," she grumbled.

Lips a hairsbreadth from her skin, Tanil whispered, "Well, you did ask him to see what he could do about getting you out of here faster." He licked and nibbled the lobe of her ear.

"Oh shut up."

"Say again, S24?"

"Not you, Dex!"

Then another voice barreled through the

console.

"And Ms. Scharsi? Hope you catch your quarry soon, beautiful. Looking forward to your return…especially if Tannie doesn't take good and frequent care of you."

A slight, almost whimsical, smile was Mr. Poacher's reward though he would never know it. Scharsi, as flattered as she was, had no qualms about making it clear she was a one-man woman.

With a chuckle, she said, "Thank you, sir, but I have complete confidence in my ability to kick ass, and Tannie's ability to make sure I'm, uh, well in hand. Commencing flight sequence. Futsuka-shi out."

"Snarky bastard."

"Oh stop growling already," Scharsi replied, though how she was able to get the words past her teeth with the big grin she wore was a mystery to her.

Chapter Nine

The con beeped three times, followed by the typically calm, though somewhat sultry voice of the ship's computer as it echoed throughout the ship.

"Deflector shields up, Commander. Entry sequence confirmed."

"Thank you."

Scharsi tightened her harness and tried to ignore the familiar whirr-snap of the ship powering up to enter the Smith Gate. It never ceased to set her teeth on edge. She'd had to engage her audio filter at the max setting to avoid the pain of the high-pitched whine that signaled the impending jump. It only lasted until the ship got up to the proper speed, a few seconds perhaps. Not long, but no less uncomfortable.

She hated this part of travel. Smith Gates were brilliant. They made travel between systems not just faster, but plain old possible. Without Smith Gates, by the time you moved from one system to another, even at warp, you'd have missed whatever event you'd traveled that far for in the first place.

The artificially pressurized, oxygen rich atmosphere inside the craft kept passengers from being affected by the twisting of space-time, but there were some things that couldn't be "technologied" away. The slight pull and pressure of passing into the wormhole of the Smiths never ceased to get under Scharsi's skin. It felt as if her entire skeleton was being pressed, then stretched. The sensation caused no pain and was nothing an ordinary human would notice, but she felt it acutely. It served as yet another reminder of her status as a walking, talking, supersensitive commodity of the IMF—a supposedly dead one, but a commodity just the same. It was also a reminder of the vastness of space. Just think, traveling faster than light through what was essentially a black hole—black hole, wormhole, whatever they wanted to call it made no difference to her. The slightest leak in the forward seals meant a silent, swift, though equally painful death. Coming through a Smith Gate alive was something Scharsi never took for granted. Ever.

Thoughts flitted through her head faster than she could analyze them. Where would the gorgeous man who shared the bridge with her go after their little mission was over? Would she ever cease to feel the dull ache of Carl's loss? How would she perform in the coming fight after being free of the craze of battle, the bloodlust of it, for seven whole years? Fuck. It was simply too much.

Godsdammit. All the thoughts about wormholes, suffocating in the black, along with the coming fight and uncertain future ushered in a wave of melancholy. Way to go, Scharsi.

It was times like this she wished she were a drinker. A bit of high grade peachy tropicure with a bit of lemon flavoring would hit the spot. Too bad she didn't have any. All there was was a protein-laden snack from the replicator — blech — and whatever was in the cold storage unit. Well, she'd just have to settle for whatever Dex had seen fit to have the crew stock them with.

"Commander?"

"Go ahead, computer." She should really get around to naming the thing. Carl used to call the ship's computer Albert. Somehow, Scharsi just couldn't quite bring herself to do the same.

"The travel plan has been updated," said the male voice.

"By whom?"

"The Web, ma'am." Ma'am? That was

different. Maybe it wasn't her imagination that there was something different about her AI unit. No doubt Dex had dinked with it along with just about everything else on this vessel.

"What is the new destination, computer?"

"Destination encrypted, course replotted."

Damn Vonner. Well, nothing to be done about it now. She'd already agreed to fly blindly to wherever they were going. These contacts Vonner was hooking her and Tanil up with had better be worth it. "Accept the new coordinates."

"Yes, Commander."

"How long before we enter the Smith?"

"The new course requires no wormhole travel, Commander. Destination reached within three to four hours."

"Fine. Take us out." A few moments later, the now-much-smoother-and-deeper voice of the male sounding computer piped up again.

"We have cleared space dock, Commander. Ready to engage warp on your command."

"Engage at warp three. Drop out of warp when we reach our destination unless hailed by law enforcement. In that event, engage security protocol S12K4."

"Yes, Commander. Engaging warp in five, four, three, two, one. Engaged."

The moment the Futsuka-shi cleared space dock headed toward wherever they were going, Scharsi flipped off the main lights and waited impatiently for the muted blue emergency lights to illuminate the path off the bridge.

Good. She may be a bit depressed, but at least she didn't have to go through a Smith Gate. A quick flick of her wrist had her harness unbuckled.

"Computer, call me if there are any issues."

"Yes, Commander."

She rose from her seat and made a beeline for the exit. Her tongue practically tasted the lillee fruit pick-me-up that she hoped awaited her in the galley.

A firm set of fingers at her waist was followed by the tight wrap of a forearm around her stomach. Tanil pulled her into his arms with a controlled strength that never ceased to impress her.

"What's wrong, Shar? Anything I can do to make it better?"

The man always managed to tell when she was upset, though her body language and expression gave away nothing. And she was sure on that point. Her ability to appear perfectly peachy just before she took someone's head off was a well-practiced skill.

"You know," he crooned quietly, knowing she had no problem picking up his barely there whisper. "I'm quite good at massage. Or I can just hold you. Tell me what you need, baby. I want to give it to you."

The moment his sentence ended, Scharsi knew exactly what she needed. Him. Period. Right now. She had no idea where this was going, knew nothing past the plan to capture this Vulf asshole and bring him back to The Web. Tanil might go on his planned vacation and chalk up their good times together as just that, a good time. She might never see him again, regardless of the impression that he wanted something more substantial and permanent from her. It wasn't her style to fret or worry. Life was what it was. The good times were good. The bad times were shit. So she would take the good memories of this time with Tanil and tuck them away to bring her smiles on the gray days.

Snuggling deeper into his embrace, Scharsi leaned her head a bit to the side so Tanil could settle his face next to hers, as was his habit whenever they stood like this.

The wall of his chest was solid and warm

against her back. With a deep breath, Scharsi pulled his unique scent deep into herself. If it were possible she'd hold that breath until the very essence of the man entered her system through the tiny blood vessels in her lungs that carried oxygen to her body. Truly breathe him in, make him a part of her forever.

He dropped a kiss on the band of muscle that connected neck to shoulder. The sigh that slipped past her lips just couldn't be helped.

"Was that a good sigh or a bad sigh."

"It was a comfy sigh."

"Yeah? What's on your mind, baby?"

"Just thinking about all the sudden changes in my life these past days. Some good. Some not so good. But this, whatever it is, with you is comfortable regardless of what happens in the days ahead. It's like a new start. Like I'm waking up from a long sleep and learning how to live again or something."

"All that, huh?"

"Yep. Can you do something for me, Tan?"

"Sure, anything."

The thought popped into her head and it didn't cross her mind to question it. And when she told him what she needed, his response was more than she could have hoped for. No hesitation. No questions. Just a simple yes.

An hour later, Scharsi stepped out of the head after a deliciously long shower. A damp towel wrapped around her body and another around her head. Tanil waited with a mixed smile on his face. He was obviously proud of his handiwork, but obviously wondered if she would like it.

"Come on and let me see already," he said. "I've never done this before and I'm dying here."

Without a word, she snatched the towel off her head and shook out her new 'do.

"Aaah, look at you. I love it."

Unable to suppress a girlish grin, she sprinted for her quarters to get a better look in the viewer. She stopped short and gingerly touched trembling fingers to her hair.

"Wow. It's, it's…"

"Yes?" Tanil pushed.

"I love it. I haven't had my hair cut since Carl rescued me from the SS labs."

Her hair was a riot of silken locks, a testament of all the DNA used to create her. Her skin was dark as cinnamon sticks, yet her hair was naturally blonde, curly, wavy, silky and thick all at once.

"It doesn't make you think of your old days in the corps, having your hair short like this again?"

"Actually, no." And she was surprised that it was true. "My hair was typically as short as the men back then."

"Yeah, but this is close," Tanil insisted.

"True, but this is a whole new me. And thank you for cutting my hair for me. I truly do love it. Can you do something else for me?"

"Anything, beautiful."

Dropping the remaining towel from around her body, it landed with a whisper on the floor at her feet. She stepped over it and into Tanil's waiting arms.

* * * * *

Just imagining the sensations that would streak along the nerve endings of her pussy sent her mind reeling with a whirlwind of possibilities—the delicious hard length of him pushing into her, separating the sleek muscles dripping with dew. Wet, soaked, ready…just for him.

She turned and ground her ass against the growing bulge beneath his black tactical pants. No doubt where the man's mind was. Good thing too, because it was the same place hers seemed to be hanging out more and more these days.

"Gods, you are just so fucking lovely." His fingers reached out to tease the soft skin underneath her breasts.

"I love when you touch me but you're not getting naked fast enough. All I've been thinking about since we took off is that wicked swirly thing you do against my clit with your tongue."

He sank a hand into her damp tresses, nails scraping lightly against her scalp just before he tightened his fingers in her hair. He tilted her head back and sank strong, white teeth into her neck right on that spot. Hot, wet tongue laved away the sting. Suck, bite, lick, over and over until she rubbed herself against him like a randwulf in heat, breathing as if she'd run a five minute kilometer. Her stomach muscles bunched and flexed along with her womb.

Gods, it was so, so good.

Before Tanil, she'd had no idea the rougher edge of sex would appeal to someone of her background. Bred to violence, she'd expected the simplest rough play to set her off like a well-timed grenade, and not in a good way. Could she snap his neck like a twig? Probably. But did she want to? Not even close. All Scharsi wanted was to submit to him, let him explore her body, let him taste, touch and tease her until her body exploded into a billion sharp-edged pieces of crystolium and diamonds. Hell, they could use her nasty fantasies to power all of Quartus Seven.

"Undress me."

She tore his clothes off. Literally. And it didn't bother her at all that the man threw his head back and laughed as she put her true strength into each movement, tearing his brand-new gear at the seams.

"I can't tell you what it does for my male ego to know that you're so hungry for my cock. And you are hungry for it, aren't you, baby?"

"Gods, yes."

"Really? How bad do you want it?" he asked as the last piece of clothing was shredded to bare his cock to her.

At first she didn't know how to put it into words. So she closed her eyes and buried her face in his groin. The hard stalk of his rod pressed against her cheek. He widened his stance on a groan as she rubbed her face over his thighs, his belly, down to nudge his full sac gently with her nose.

"I want you to fuck me. I want it so bad my

pussy is swollen and wet, throbbing, aching. Gods, I want you buried in me, taking me, owning me as you do every time. At the same time I want to take you down my throat, to lick you, taste you. Gods, Tan, no one tastes like you. I just want to savor it on my tongue, but I don't have the patience I need to lick you properly. Give it to me. Hard, deep. That's what I want."

"Wow. All that, huh?"

But he panted for her as wildly as she did for him. Oh yes. Bring it.

"Hard and deep, Scharsi?"

"Oh yes. Hard and deep. You know how I like it. And I'm glad to be able to say such a thing."

"On the bed. Head down."

Oh she knew the words to this particular song, all right. And she was happy to sing it loud and often. Up on the bed, the soft covers whispered over the skin on her knees as she knelt. Her shoulders welcomed the same caress of synthsilk as her shoulders met the mattress.

"Reach back and spread yourself for me. Show me that pretty pussy. Show me you're mine."

Scharsi's fingers slid along her outer folds, the skin so slick from her own dew it was a challenge to get a good hold. Finally her fingers made purchase. The moment she'd spread her pussy lips, the head of his cock was there, hot, almost scalding as he pressed in.

Only halfway in, she was begging.

"Oh yes. Yes. Please. Give it to me."

Then he was seated, filling her just this side of too much. He groaned as his cock flexed inside of her. The muscled channel of her pussy responded with a flex of its own. Amazing how her body pulled at his, all on its own, out of her control.

He slid back and out until the head of his cock caught on the tight ringed entrance of her sheath. Then he moved with a particularly deep dig that made her push her hips back at him, seeking, needing more of that perfect girth as it parted her slick tightening folds. Until the nerve endings fired and fired again. Until she came so hard it ripped her inside out. Until she could do nothing but give it all up with something she'd never done in pleasure—scream.

Slowly Tanil pulled out and sat back on his knees. Scharsi rolled over and took in the lines of his body. Her gaze landed on his cock, shiny with her dew. The scent of their loving filled the air. It reminded Scharsi of sweet summer fields on Trescalane just as the red coffee and tropical fruits were harvested for the season's production of strong javé and potent liqueur. And he was just so comfortable in his skin, comfortable with her. He gave her his trust, which is something she'd never received from another person in all her life, save one.

Tanil wrapped himself around her and buried his nose in her hair, as was his habit.

"You were a knockout before, but this new short and sassy hairdo of yours is off the charts in the sexy department."

It would have been completely dry by now if not for the new drenching of sweat—all his fault of course. Not that she was complaining. Instead of a comment, Scharsi yawned big and so unladylike she almost snorted as she snuggled closer.

Her stomach rumbled and gurgled like an old derelict ship that had run out of fuel. She could still use that snack she'd been headed to before the haircut, shower and being waylaid— boy had she ever been laid—by Tanil. She'd been three kinds of depressed at what seemed like eons ago, but now that her attitude had been properly adjusted and her muscles all languified, a nap seemed more in order, whether her gut rolled around in protest of its lack of food or not.

So, any idea where we're going?"

"Not a clue," she replied on yet another yawn. "All I know is that Vonner said the place we're going is some super seekrit resistance hole up."

"Seekrit?" Tanil laughed so hard her head bounced up and down on his shoulder. "Snark much, Scharsi?"

She smiled. Couldn't help it. "Well, anyway," she drawled, "Dex programmed the coordinates and in a few hours we'll end up wherever it is we're supposed to be."

"Sounds easy enough. Aw hell, sorry, be right back."

A few moments later, Tanil returned, flopping down next to her as if he'd known her forever, like they were truly a couple and not just sleeping together. The warm towel he'd run to the head to get was placed gently between her legs as he cleaned her up. No awkward movements, no weird silence. Just lovely comfort.

The towel sailed across the room toward the pile of towels she'd used on her hair and body.

The man dropped a kiss on her shoulder, smiled and wrapped her up in his arms again.

When he let out a contented sigh, Scharsi lost it.

The alarm on Tanil's face at her first sob would have had her cracking up if not for the soul-deep emotion that bubbled over inside her. If only he knew what he'd done. She hadn't been so completely exposed, so torn down, yet emotionally built up, and all by his openness, his desire to see to her needs and the willingness to accept her, flaws and all.

"Oh Gods, baby what is it? Did I hurt you? I'm so sorry."

A loud hiccup and a round of all-out bawling had her shoulders shaking and nose running as the tears flowed. "No, I'm fine."

"Fine? Are you fucking kidding me? You're crying, Scharsi."

Chapter Ten

Heart lodged in his throat, Tanil gathered Scharsi close and spoke what he hoped were soothing words against her ear, careful to keep his tone low in case her auditory filter was disengaged.

"Tell me what's wrong. I'm a tough guy and all, but I don't think I can take too many tears from you. It breaks my heart."

"It's just that…" She stopped short on a loud slurpy sniff. Completely unladylike and the cutest thing Tanil had ever seen.

"I mean, you're just so easy to be with. No drama. No weirdness about what I am. No regrets about what you are, I mean, being a soldier for the fucking Amalgamation and all. You care about me, Tan. I mean really care. I can tell by the way you touch me. The way you listen to me when I have something to say. The way you make me laugh to the point my stomach hurts."

And it was true. He did care about her. In fact, he was far gone in love with the woman. He hadn't told her because he didn't want to distract her or take her focus off the hunt. This was dangerous stuff and the last thing Scharsi needed was a man-sized distraction on the way into a life-or-death situation. Yet at the same time, the way her tears flowed, the expression on her beautiful face all looked a lot like love too.

With each passing day he found himself craving to be the one constant in Scharsi's life. Did she love him? Maybe. Maybe not. But he was determined to be the best thing in her life until she decided that she needed, wanted, someone other than him.

This tough-as-nails woman was bred to violence, yet could sit here and cry with him, laugh at his dumb jokes while making a few terribly corny ones herself. She was smart as a whip, wise as an old woman, yet when time allowed, as carefree as a kid who enjoyed candy and a tickle on the tummy. Well rounded should have been her middle name. What more could a man ask for? Well, he could think of one thing.

"Scharsi, please don't cry."

"I can't help it. You just make me so happy. And I know I've said it a million times, but you make me comfortable. I was already comfortable in my own skin, but I've never been with anyone who made me feel so…normal."

"Would it make you feel even more normal for me to tell you that I love you?" Damn it. He hadn't meant to say it. Hadn't he just finished telling himself she didn't need such a distraction? But, it just slipped out.

"What? You love me?"

"I do. I love everything about you."

Tanil was puzzled when she turned away and lowered her lashes. Scharsi didn't have a shy bone in her body. What was this about?

"Scharsi, look at me."

She shook her head no.

No?

"Don't get me wrong, Tan. I love myself, love who I am. It's just that, well, it's different to have someone else love me this way. Carl was the only one, and even he didn't quite love me like this. I don't know if that makes sense to you but…"

Then it dawned on him—there was a part of herself she held back, a piece that was specific to what she was rather than who she was. Something he hadn't seen until now, but was of so little consequence Tanil hadn't given it a second thought. Obviously, Scharsi had given it a second, third and probably a fourth thought. But why? Did the woman think he hadn't already accepted it? Of course it was a ridiculous notion, but his Scharsi bordered on "emotional wreck" just now, so perhaps he'd let it go, right? No way in hell.

Quietly, in a tone he hoped was sweet, he said, "Let me see you, Scharsi. Please."

At her hesitation he added, "Scharsi, please look at me, sweetheart. Share that last bit of yourself with me. Besides it's only fair."

She turned with a half smile and a questioning tilt of her head.

"Well, you know that my birthmark is just under the curve of my ass. It's only fair I get to see your birthmark."

He knew she understood. Super Soldiers might incur a scar from a battle or two, but they were born perfect. No birthmarks or any other physical flaw. Except one that, regardless of the decades of research and DNA manipulation, the Military Sciences Lab couldn't breed away.

"Come on, baby. Give it to me."

Lifting her head, she stared him straight in the eye. Like the subtle shifting of dusk to dawn, Scharsi's honey brown irises began to fade until a silvery white gaze peered boldly back at him. She was still the slightest unsure—he could see it in her body language, the stiffness of her spine, the tightness around her mouth. Tanil couldn't blame her after all she'd been through, but he was certainly determined to wipe it from her mind.

"Beautiful, Scharsi. They're beautiful, just like all the rest of you."

Her expression was dubious at best. He looked closer, could see the iris begin to darken.

"No, don't. Don't change them back. I love your eyes."

Reluctantly she relented and allowed that slight hint of brown to retreat, leaving the most beautiful moonlight-colored eyes Tanil had ever seen. He'd done his share of work with SS, but he couldn't think of a single one with eyes quite like his Scharsi's. Deeply expressive, they told of her struggles and her determination to survive. Her zest for life, though she'd spent many years hiding, her loyalty to those she cared for and a bone-deep honor and commitment to doing what was right. But when she tilted her head just so, he caught the glimpse of what he was truly looking for—the passionate, giving lover that reveled in not only her femininity, but her strength as well. Oh, and orgasms. Yes, the woman did love to come, for sure.

"Now what?" she asked.

Guiding the conversation, Tanil let his curiosity shine through. He had no doubt Scharsi would appreciate knowing his true thoughts. Besides, she deserved this from him rather than some fake or formulated response just to put her at ease.

"Every SS I ever worked with had those telltale opaque grayish eyes. I honestly thought you were wearing contacts to make your eyes such a pretty honey brown. How is it you can change them at will?"

"Carl made them for me. They're lenses, yes, but he made them with nanites. It was one of the experiments he was working on when he formulated the plan to rescue me from being terminated. It's actually the nanites that change color and not the lens itself. All I send is a small electric pulse, similar to the one I send to my auditory filter that allows me to modify the volume at will. I can instruct them to darken or lighten. Basically, I can turn them on and off."

"That's amazing. I knew the technology existed, but had no idea it was out of the lab."

"It wasn't out of the lab. Someone else may have picked up where Carl left off, but he took his research with him when we fled Earth. I imagine they weren't happy to have to start from scratch. So you like the honey brown, eh?"

"I like you, period. I love your eyes no matter what color you choose to have them. I enjoy everything about you from head to toe, that includes the parts of you that you may believe make you less than human. I love it all. Understand?"

Her smile, though just a tease of a grin really, made him all warm inside. "That's better. Now how's about a kiss, gorgeous?"

It was a sweet, slow nibble meant to relax rather than inflame. And it felt like coming home.

As Tanil's lips met Scharsi's, the computer interrupted. Interesting. It seemed to be doing a lot of that lately. Damn machine.

"Commander, we are approaching our destination."

"You know, I swear Dex did something to the computer's voice," Tanil said.

"Why do you say that?" Scharsi turned over and buried her face in Tanil's neck as she reached for sleep. Since they had no idea where they were going, it could be hours before they dropped out of warp. Could even be a day or two.

"He sounds way sexier than the AI I

remember when I first came on board. That voice was bland, flat. Definitely unsexy."

Scharsi giggled and snuggled in closer. Mmmm. Tanil liked her in this position. He liked her on her back, or on her knees, bare ass in the air, up against the wall. But he also enjoyed this light, sweet whatever-it-was as she laid her head on his shoulder and sighed contentedly.

Proximity alert! Proximity alert! Sirens sounded as the words blared throughout the ship.

"Holy shit!" Sprinting naked from the bed, Scharsi logged into the nearest access point on the wall near the door to her quarters. "Computer, what the hell is going on?"

"We are entering the atmosphere…"

"Atmosphere of where?"

"The Quantinium Moon that orbits the planet Mimnet, Commander. Autopilot will be disengaged in six minutes."

"Couldn't you have given me more warning than this?" she snapped.

"I am sorry, Commander, I am not programmed to analyze rhetorical questions."

Fucking smart-assed computer.

"Wait until I get my hands on Vonner. What the hell was he thinking by having me agree to fly blindly into this?"

Tanil literally jumped into his clothes while moving toward the door. Scharsi didn't bother. It would take her almost two minutes to get all the way back to the bridge. She had no time for modesty. It was the one disadvantage to having a large med ship. It had been converted into a fighting machine, but that didn't change the size of the damn thing.

"What's going on? What's happening?" Tanil ran right behind her.

"The ship's computer can't handle getting us on the ground. Have you ever been to Mimnet?"

"Once. I don't remember much of it. I got so airsick from all the turbul…ah shit!"

"Exactly. The turbulence. Mimnet is bad enough, but the computer said we're coming up on Quantinium Moon. Landing on Mimnet itself might be a rocky proposition, but Quantinium is ten times as tricky."

"Well at least I get a nice view of your ass while you run to save the ship."

"Perv."

"Definitely."

Scharsi settled into the captain's chair. Tanil ran back to her bunk, grabbed some clothes, then held tightly to the controls as she hopped up and dressed at record speed. Seated again, Scharsi thanked the Gods for her unusual strength. Piloting this craft through to the moon was a fucking fighting match — her against the atmosphere.

Tanil took the co-chair and brought up the topography grid. "Good Gods. Is there really something in this place? Scanners are coming up empty."

"Must be or Vonner wouldn't have sent us here."

"Trust him that much, do you?"

"Actually, I do," Scharsi said. "Men like him have their own code of conduct. Once they bring you into the fold, people like Ulric Vonner will treat you like family. Once we became BHI good guys, we became part of his crew."

"Well, I don't know about you, but you don't send family into this kind of shit without warning." Tanil grimaced as he held onto the arms of his chair for dear life.

"Yeah, but think about it this way, Tan, the people he's sending us to hook up with are part of that family. He's not going to out them just to make it easier for us to get to them. He has to protect them just as he would protect us. Period."

"Makes sense. So now explain why it feels like my teeth are being rattled around in my head by this Gods-awful turbulence? If it keeps up, I'll be painting the bridge floor with all kinds of new smelly colors."

"The ice storms are bad enough, but the ground isn't much better. Computer, magnify distance to thirty percent."

"Yes, Commander."

After a wicked drop in altitude, Scharsi pulled back on the controls to level them out. "See, look there. This place is one big mountain range covered with nothing but jagged peaks and a hell of a lot of snow and ice. One wrong move and we not only risk a nasty crash, but also being spotted by one of a bazillion sensors floating around in the black."

"And we're going there on purpose?"

"Looks like. Computer, disengage autopilot on my mark."

"What? Disengage?" Yep, he was definitely going to blow chunks.

"There's no choice but to pilot without the benefit of the computer's quick calculations. Computer, five, four, three, two. Mark."

"Autopilot disengaged, Commander."

"Oh lord, we're gonna die."

"Oh stop," Scharsi said playfully. "Thankfully this is an agile craft with good maneuverability."

"Yeah, but she sure has a big ass," Tanil grumbled.

"I thought you liked big asses."

What could he say to that? It was beyond the truth, and Scharsi's was a spankable piece of art that was permanently framed in his mind. He was a happy man. A nauseated one, but happy none the less.

Scharsi laughed at his silence.

"Don't worry. I'll get us down in one piece. Besides, if we die now, we won't be able to avenge you and Carl. Oh, and I'd really miss all the lovely sex and hugs and stuff too."

"Great timing for snark, woman."

Another wild drop was followed by what felt like someone batting the ship off to the left again.

Tanil felt like a little kid when he asked, "Are we there yet?"

"Computer, any readings on the short-range sensors? We should be close enough to where we're going to at least pick up some signs of life."

"Negative, Commander."

Tanil's forehead tensed. He turned to find Scharsi with the same expression painted on her lovely face. Tanil could practically hear her brain working out the scenario. They'd been sent to a place to meet people, but there were no signs of life.

The ship lurched, fell, then climbed again. Fuck. Tanil held his breath and tried to keep his stomach from turning inside out.

"Computer, what is the composition of Quantinium, including atmosphere?"

"One moment, Commander."

Mere seconds ticked by. Felt like a Godsdamn eon.

"The atmosphere is unbreathable. Air temperature fluctuates between minus one hundred and minus one hundred fifty. There is no life form that can survive such temperatures. However, the high mineral content of the soil would interfere with my ability to get a clear reading if there were any life. Sensors are ineffective, Commander."

"Sensors are useless? Would that also include any sensors orbiting Mimnet?"

"That is correct, Commander."

"Brilliant. Simply brilliant."

"What's brilliant? The fact that my gut is

flipping inside out in ten-second intervals?"

"No. Putting a base here. The computer's calculations are correct. We're here. I just need to drop down a bit more to get out of the worst of the air currents smacking the ship around."

Tanil sat up straighter to look down at the quickly approaching planet. "Hey look, the whole place is under an energy dome. No wonder the ship's sensors didn't pick it up."

"There's probably more built under the moon's surface as well. That would protect the people here in the event the dome failed."

"We are being hailed, Commander."

"Respond using whatever protocol Vonner had Dex give you. Inform our hosts we'll be on the ground in less than four minutes."

"Yes, Commander."

* * * * *

Kev lay at the bottom of the muddy incline, a slight smile on his face as the life blood gushed from his body. Yes, he'd been left for dead. He'd known it would come to this. It was the only logical conclusion the moment he realized what he had to do. He'd lied to the Amalgamation. And if all was going according to plan, Captain Tanil and the renegade Gen8 were carrying out their mission, a mission those he answered to had put into motion.

Disengaging his auditory filter, the Super Soldier let the sounds of the dawning day wash through him.

Vulf. Pompous bastard. He hadn't even waited until nighttime to leave Kev for dead. Nope, just had his cohorts drag him here in the light of a new day. He briefly wondered where "here" was. Wherever it was, the suns were rising beautifully. It was humid, the air thick, but clean. Flat on his back, he took in a deep breath, drawing the scent of the foliage and thick brush that grew along the edge of the pit. Something that smelled like wet fur rustled off in the distance.

It would be hot today, though the mist clinging to the vegetation was cool and dewy still. A howl caught his attention, but he didn't worry. The beasts wouldn't come for him just yet. By the time they figured out that fresh meat had been tossed into their midst he'd be long dead. At least he hoped so. The wound was certainly severe enough and feeling was quickly abandoning his limbs. Yet he was a Super Soldier. Highly advanced reengineered DNA ruled his body and for the first time he hoped he didn't heal faster than his wounds could kill him.

He'd shot Captain Tanil Taikiji just as he'd been ordered to by the Amalgamation puppet who, in turn, had him tossed in this pit. But no one other than his true superiors would ever know that he'd intentionally missed the vital organs that would have given the dear captain mere moments to live. Nor would it ever be revealed that the tell-tale clues left behind at the crime scene for the Gen8 SS to later find had not been simple carelessness of a team of soldiers with more confidence than brains. And the secret would go with him to his grave. And it would go there today.

The Gen8's secured file indicated that her specialty was reasoning and analytics. That, joined with what Tanil knew of the Amalgamation's special "medical research" plan, meant that the female Gen8 and her ex-Amalgamation partner had figured it all out by now. And if his calculations were correct, they'd started down the path of carrying out his handler's plan. If the female was as tenacious about revenge as she'd been about staying hidden for seven years, the two were well on their way to exposing the Amalgamation's efforts to spread diseases that hadn't been seen in humanoids in almost a millennia.

Strangely how Kev's logical brain still ruled him. He'd thought that at a moment like this, where departing from this plane was imminent, that the emotions he'd been trained to suppress since he was old enough to walk and talk would come bursting forth. Death was an emotional subject to all humanoids, right? Yet, there was nothing. No panic. No regret. Just a calm acceptance that he'd done what was logically sound for the survival of the species and nothing else mattered. And for once in his life, Kev wished he gave a good Godsdamn about something other than doing the expedient thing.

Chapter Eleven

Within moments of disembarking the Futsuka-shi, Scharsi and Tanil were escorted from the ship and through the surprisingly large base. She'd expected a few hundred rebels and pirates here fighting with the rebellion. Shocked shitless was mild compared to what she'd truly felt upon encountering several thousands jammed into the reception bay, all eager to get a look at the new guests.

Though Scharsi and Tanil were flanked on all sides by mean-looking escorts armed to the teeth, Scharsi forced her hands to relax. Though covered in a thick black jumpsuit and well-insulated overcloak to ward off the cold, the better part of wisdom required her to leave her weapons aboard ship rather than take advantage of all the hiding places in her clothing. The result—she felt naked. Hell, even on Ukure, traveling back and forth to her old desk job at the Space Port, she'd always carried some kind of weapon hidden on her body. But not today. Word had it that two SS were consorts of the Princess Cerise. Even the notorious pirate,

Regan, who'd terrorized and blown up more Amalgamation freighters and ships in the last ten years than anyone alive, was rumored to be a Super Soldier.

Most didn't believe it. After all, no one simply stopped being a soldier for the IMF. No simply left the corps. The only way out was dead...or at least that was the rumor.

Regardless of what was rumor and what was fact, if she and Tanil were going to get their help she had to do something to earn their trust, like walking into the midst of a throng of thankfully well-behaved unknowns without a single blade, laser pistol, staff or other hardware anywhere on her person. She hoped the gesture didn't go unnoticed.

Out of the larger gathering areas they moved quietly through several long, surprisingly well-lit corridors. After endless left and right turns they stopped at a nondescript door and were ushered into a large, though windowless, room. An itty-bitty woman flanked, actually more like dwarfed, by two huge male humanoids stood waiting behind a big old-fashioned desk. Interesting. The thing looked like real wood. Strange to see such a relic in the midst of all the concrete, steel and weatherproofed glass and plastic panes of the hidden base.

Their escort ducked out of the room, leaving them alone. Scharsi tilted her head and took a closer look. Based on the description she'd been given, this was the Princess Cerise. She was short with a head full of glossy dark hair that framed a lovely face. Her eyes were definitely her most prominent feature, so large they almost seemed too large for her face and made her appear fairytale-like. Scharsi wondered if all Carnelian princesses had purple irises. Were they all so little and cute?

Good thing I'm comfortable with who I am or she'd make me feel like a lumbering heifer.

"Hi, I'm Cerise. This is Tie and Regan, my consorts. We lead the resistance in this quadrant, or what there is left of it."

"My name is Scharsi, former Senior Commander, Special Weapons and Tactics. This is Tanil, formerly an Amalgamation…" was as far as she got.

Practically hiding the Princess, Regan and Tie's postures morphed from calm-and-in-control into protect-and-serve mode as they eyed Tanil like a horde of Amalgamation officers were going to crawl out of his ass to arrest them all.

"I'm sure you understand what this means." Scharsi gestured with her head toward her empty holsters and missing weapons belt, careful not to move her hands away from her body in any way. "We have good reasons for coming here." She held her temper and spoke calmly while still subtly inserting herself between Tanil and the mean-assed, bald, and damn-near-growling Regan and his oversized partner, Tie.

If Regan pulled his brows down to scowl any harder, the skin on his face would pull against his cheekbones tight enough to split and bleed. The tank called Tie was no better. They were SS, for sure. The body structure and silver eyes gave them away. Even without knowing what kind of training they endured or how long they'd been in the program before they managed to escape, one fact was incontrovertible — there was no way she could take both of them. One at a time, surely. But both? No fucking way.

Without thought, she calculated the exact moves to take them down, given size, distance and lack of weapons. She knew that if she had to, she could at least hurt one of them before they took her out, giving Tanil precious seconds to get the hell out of point-blank range.

Gods please don't let it come to that. The
prayer to the Universe lasted all of four seconds,
four loooonnngggg seconds as they eyed Tanil,
maintaining less than hospitable body language.
Scharsi's patience started to slip. She simply
would not stand for letting these two big-assed
clones—Gods she must really be pissed off to
even think such a derogatory word—threaten
her man. And obviously Tanil had the same
idea.

Tanil boldly stepped in front of Scharsi with
an agility that sent her awe of him up a few
notches. He was the second person ever in her
whole life to try to protect her. And he wasn't
bluffing or fucking around when he looked up
almost ten centimeters into the silvery-white
eyes of two surprised male Super Soldiers and
snarled at them.

Scharsi almost took her focus off the
immediate potential threat to gape at Tanil for
such a sweet gesture. But it was a gesture that
could get him killed. Fast.

A tiny finger poked Regan in the chest while
another grabbed Tie by the ear, and none too
gently.

"Oh cut it out, you two," Cerise snapped.
She was obviously the civil one in the bunch. She

stepped forward, handed Tanil a glass of what was surely an illegal brand of whiskey and asked him a simple, point-blank question. No snarling. No posturing. Just a common sense question. Scharsi decided she liked the itty-bitty princess, even if she did make Scharsi feel like a great big herd animal.

"I heard you were almost killed." Vonner. Had to have been Vonner who let that one slip. "So what do you have on the Amalgamation that made them turn on one of their own?" Cerise asked. Tanil didn't hesitate.

"I've got major dirt on their latest scientific operation."

Tie cut him off. "If you think we're just going to…"

"Tie, the man was in the middle of a sentence. Sorry, Captain Tanil. Please continue," Cerise said. Regan hadn't said a word. Perhaps he was the calm one of the pair, but the sharp glint in his eye told Scharsi he'd try to take their heads off if their story didn't check out.

Tanil continued as if he'd never been interrupted.

"The Military Sciences Lab, under the direction of the IMF, has ported the older defective Super Soldier DNA from generations one and two into ordinary people, even humanoids of other species."

"What? Are you fucking kidding me?" This from Tie, who wore a thunderous expression mixed with horror at the thought of what this could mean.

"No joke. This is as real as it gets," Scharsi said. With a nod toward Tanil, the man continued.

"Just as gene therapy was used to eliminate certain diseases and undesirable traits out of the SS, reverse engineering that same gene therapy can reintroduce those diseases. Vaccines for these bugs don't exist. The diseases were wiped out so long ago no one thought there was any reason to continue producing vaccine for things that didn't exist. Now the goal is to try to reintroduce some of the more horrific diseases that were annihilated back then."

"But, but why?" Cerise's expression contained mere curiosity, but her body language screamed "pissed off".

"Think about it," Tanil said. "The only cures are being developed by the IMF, simply because they must have the ability to cure the diseases they create, otherwise it would quickly become a pandemic. And since the IMF have the cures, that means anyone infected must dance to their tune. This medical "research" was forced on nonmilitary personnel, carried out without consent, and sometimes without their knowledge. Then the bastards planted those people among the general population, particularly among the pirates."

"But why would they go through all of this?" Cerise asked, genuinely perplexed.

"Basically to bring down the rebel factions. Think about it, baby," said Regan. "If the rebels and pirates are eliminated there is no rebellion. And even if we aren't all wiped out, if an infected person wants to get uninfected they'll have to give the Amalgamation something valuable enough to trade for the vaccines and cures. Any guesses on what that might be?"

"Yep. The location of rebel bases, the names of people they do business with, pirate hideouts. You name it," Tie said.

"Exactly. But if this kind of information got out, that the government was infecting its own people..." Cerise's words trailed off as she shook her head in utter disbelief.

Regan growled, "Godsdamn germ warfare all over again. We know they're capable of some lowdown schemes, but even I can't believe they'd stoop so low. I mean, fuck, these people weren't even given a choice to be lab rats."

"Why can't you believe it? They created SS and gave you no choice as to whether you wanted to be one." Tanil motioned to the three former Super Soldiers.

Tie almost looked sorry for his behavior. Almost. After a bit of silence, he spoke for the group. "Well, he's got a damn good point there. So, what the hell are we going to do about it?"

A diabolical twist of Regan's lips accompanied by a calculating gleam in his crystalline white eyes sent a frisson of fear through Tanil until he remembered these guys were on his side. Thank the Gods. In fact he silently thanked every God he could think of.

"Well, I think the resistance has found a new way to thwart the Amalgamation and help our people all at the same time." With a questioning dip of both Cerise and Tai's eyebrows, Regan smiled wide and said, "The pirates, of which we have no knowledge of…" The snark was unmistakable since Regan was the HPIC—the head pirate in charge. "I think they'd be willing to assist us in relieving the Amalgamation bastards of their new goods—the vaccine for their living hell. We can inoc our people and anyone else the Amalgamation bastards thought they could use against us. The rest would be worth a fortune on the market, don't you think?"

"You mean get to them before the Amalgamation does, give them the cure and win them to our side?" Cerise asked. "Brilliant."

Tie added, "And it doesn't matter where they have it stowed, I'll find it. It'll be well guarded. I hope the bastards don't whine about the uneven odds of us against them."

"While we're at it, I can collect a bounty on the asshole who ordered Carl's murder and tried to take out Tanil."

"Let me guess," said Tie. "They wanted Tanil out of the way because he knows who is at the center of this whole death-and-disease thing, right?"

At Tanil's nod, Tie said, "Yep. Oldest trick in the book. You'd think these guys would come up with original ideas for wanting to assassinate someone by now."

Regan headed for the door, his step sure yet eager. It was obvious the man was ready to get it on. "I'll get the wheels turning, starting with confirmation of folks getting sick for no reason, who they are, where they are, and whether they've been picked up by the IMF."

Tie joined him. "And I'll find out where…what's his name?"

"Vulf. Vulf Destry. He's a lieutenant colonel, 28th CyberSEALDivision. Couple of ranks above me, though we both reported to Brigadier General Sachus. I'm pretty sure Vulf pulled the strings that led to my near-death experience. He must have found out that I'd gotten the skinny on the reintroduction program. But Vulf is an authority, not a SS handler. The only reason he has access to any Super Soldiers is because he picked the ones that were the first guinea pigs in the sick research program."

Tie wrinkled his nose and said, "Vulf? His name is Vulf? Are you serious? Sounds like some kinda slang for vomit. You just tell me when you want to grab him and I'll point you in the right direction. Let's just hope he's off-planet and not at Amalgamation headquarters on Aboo-Two."

"It doesn't matter where he is. He's a dead man walking."

Tanil turned at the sound of his lover's voice. Scharsi's grin was as coldly calculating as her male counterparts. Pride bloomed in his chest.

These soldiers had just, with only a few words, revealed the lengths they were willing to go to for their people. They would do anything, take any risk…and kick any ass.

* * * * *

Scharsi felt absolutely pretty, something she hadn't experienced in a long time. Feeling sexy in Tanil's arms every night was quite different from feeling sexy in her clothes in the daytime. After all, there was very little sexy about a BHI black-on-black tactical uniform. Sure it fit her body as it should, but it wasn't made to show off her curves and certainly wasn't suitable as bedroom attire.

Today's outfit, a gift from Princess Cerise, was a wholly feminine affair. Well, almost. Cerise had revealed that the bottoms were made of a synthsilk fabric so light that it would practically float against her skin as she moved. The cut was such that it looked like an elegant skirt, but the panel in the front actually hid the true design — a pair of wide-legged pants to give her the ability to move quickly and fight, if needed.

The top was a finely knit material, soft and clingy and just thick enough to keep the chill off her arms. It fit like a second skin, showing off her breasts, the muscular set of her shoulders and back, clear down to the flare of her waist. Where the top ended was where the pants began.

Both were done in a jewel-toned green that reminded Scharsi of precious stones. But she still sported tactical boots. After all, comfort was comfort.

"Hey, beautiful, how 'bout joining me and my friends here for a drank?"

Drank? Did the man actually say "drank"? Good grief. Guess it took all kinds to make a rebellion work. And these men sported baggy overall suits that, regardless of the oversizing, still didn't quite fit. These guys were simply…big. Not muscular, but tall and wide with bellies that could probably use a few jackknife sit-ups. They sported various splotches of what looked like crystolium dust and engine grease. Hmmm. Scharsi wondered what use engine grease could possibly be in one's hair.

"No thanks. Appreciate the offer."

"Aw come on, darlin'. We're about the only ones here that ain't a-scared of you. Take your pleasure where you can git it."

"I will say this once and once only. Go. Away."

With that, Scharsi turned her back on the man and his dumb-as-volcanic-ash friends and went back to choosing a gift for Tanil. It was a hard thing. She wasn't really sure what he liked. Today was an open market of sorts. Those who wanted to sell or trade brought their wares to the Bay, a large empty central space in the main hangar. Luckily there was plenty to choose from.

Idiot Number One stepped into her path.

"Word has it you're some big bad Super Soldier bitch. But we know better."

"Yeah, we know better," said Idiot One's sidekick. "Everybody knows that no Super Soldier leaves the corps. Only ones ever done it is the consorts of the princess."

Scharsi smiled as she recalled Carl getting a friend to hack into the IMF security files. What she'd read about her generation of SS blew her away. It happened years ago, but just the thought of what they'd found in that file made her chest swell with pride. Why? Because it was the truth, probably the only truth she'd ever seen come out of the IMF.

CONFIDENTIAL—Conclusion of Gen8 Testing: Ability to heal has increased significantly compared to a typical human. E.g. A bullet wound to a human's deep muscle tissue of the shoulder would require 840 hours, or 35 standard days, of intense physical therapy and rehabilitation. For the same wound, Gen8 requires approximately 210 hours, or 9 days with no intense therapy. Gen8 is vulnerable to fatality by puncturing the heart, intestines or brain. However, the increased bone density in the skull makes it difficult. If a Gen8 soldier decided to turn on the IMF there would be little we could do to stop them, other than track them down and kill them. Quelling a rebellion could only be accomplished by breeding a more advanced soldier.

"Why don't you show us how badass you are? Come on back to our room. Bet you taste like real chocolate with all that pretty dark skin."

Scharsi looked down at the fingers now dirtying up the sleeve of her new outfit. Asshole.

"Take your hand off me. I won't tell you again."

He didn't. Bad choice.

"Well, you just look like a big-assed dike, to me. And a dike ain't nothin' but a wannabe man."

Out of the corner of her eye, Scharsi saw a familiar shape on the edge of the growing crowd. Tanil. He simply shook his head with an expression of pity. She knew it wasn't for her, but for the mouth breather who threw back his head and laughed like he'd told the biggest joke of the century. What the oversized, engine-grease-wearing IQ-deficient backward acting human didn't realize was that he was the joke. If he pushed her hard enough, took one more step, he would learn that some jokes had terrible punch lines.

Damn. He took a step. Too bad.

Tanil had just left a meeting with Regan to discuss their next move. A shortcut through the central square brought him up on a scene that he had a feeling would become all too familiar.

He overheard the greaseball who had the nerve to touch Scharsi. All he could do was shake his head in amazement at how stupid some people really were. In fact, Tanil wondered where the man got the brain energy to breathe everyday. Before he could complete the thought, Scharsi was in action.

The woman spun off her weak foot and took down the target so fast Tanil was glad she wasn't mad at him. Her aim for the soft flesh of the man's belly had been true and he could tell she hadn't bothered to temper the force behind her perfectly executed spinning back kick.

To this point, he'd only seen this woman's purely feminine side. This? This was something else entirely. This was the trained soldier. The woman who could put her fist through a body and pull out a beating heart. The thought made him absently rub the healed laser rifle wound, now nothing more than a fading scar on his chest.

Her opponent, if you could call him that, must have thought Scharsi was through with him. Instead she raised the bawling, writhing mass of "supposed male" off the paved deck and tossed him into one of his buddies who probably thought he was coming to the rescue. Poor suckers.

The next idiot swung a metal pipe at her. She not only blocked it, but twisted her wrist at the last moment, wrapped her fingers around the shaft, snatched it out of the guy's hand and conked him in the forehead with it. A resounding crack filled the silence of the gathering crowd, followed by oooh's and a few aaah's, mostly female, as the guy keeled over and was out for the count.

One little girl close to Tanil even whispered, "Mom, can I learn to fight like her? Kirby Dashe always picks on me and I'd like to thrash him. Can I, Mom? Please?"

The last and final brainless wonder rushed Scharsi from behind. She grabbed the hand from around her neck and with a flick her wrist, the man found himself twirled around with his back against Scharsi's front in a sleeper hold. In seconds, he slid to the floor and landed like a sack of rocks on the ground, out for the count.

It was over so fast that if Tanil hadn't been there he wouldn't have believed it had happened at all. Well, that and the small pile of bodies moaning and rolling around on the ground, each one desperately holding onto various body parts.

Scharsi looked up at him with an expression of horror, as if she couldn't believe what she'd done. Or as if she was afraid at what he might think or do now that he'd seen what she was capable of. She had, in fact, tossed those men around like they were little more than a few gear bags that needed putting away.

Tanil let the grin he'd been suppressing spread across his lips. He was damn proud of her at that moment. She'd needed to protect herself and hadn't hesitated to do so. Besides, the thought of his hellion in a fight and coming out on top relaxed a tension in his gut that he hadn't realized was truly there—concern for her getting hurt in the little mission they were about to undertake.

She caught his gaze, held it, visibly relaxed and removed her foot from another perp's neck.

Tanil moved toward her with purpose, still wearing that shit-eating grin. What the hell was he up to?

Without breaking stride, he picked her up—which was no small feat—and tossed her over one shoulder. The small crowd that had gathered when the brick-headed pirate wannabes had tried to touch her uninvited now gawked at Tanil, their eyes alight with wonder.

"Look, he just walked right over and snatched her up off the ground," one woman said.

"Yeah, and she didn't even deck him or nothing." This from one of the semiconscious men's friends.

"Guess she's particular about who gets to play with all that beautiful skin." Wow, now that was unexpected, especially coming from the man whose neck had just spent a few uncomfortable moments stretched beneath her boots.

"Tanil, put me…"

"Stop squirming or you'll fall."

"I can handle a little fall from this height. Now put me the fuck down." She started to struggle, but before she could get her hips moving enough to dislodge herself from her unexpected perch…

"I said, stay still, Shar."

Smack!

"Oh. My. Gods. Did you just spank me?"

His hand smoothed over her ass in a purely carnal caress, soothing the sting.

"Yep. Did you like it?"

"I. Well, uh."

"Well, if you're not sure, let's try it again."

Smack!

"Oh fuck," she gasped. Yep, she liked it. Especially when his hand traveled from her warming ass to the crease between her cheeks to stroke, stroke, stroke.

"One more for good measure?"

"Oh yes."

Smack!

It felt so good she didn't even bother asking where they were going.

Chapter Twelve

Naked and sweating, Scharsi felt like a veritable feast laid out for Tanil's pleasure. Like a new land ready to be explored, excavated for the finding of lost treasure. Her stomach muscles burned from constantly contracting as Tanil wrung long, wild, all-consuming orgasms from her. So far she'd survived two—one from his mouth as he gobbled up her pussy, the other from his fingers tap-tap-tapping her clit as he kissed her all over.

Gods, the man was a connoisseur of pussy. But her body was empty. She needed the intimacy and emotional bond that only sex with the one you loved could cement.

"Fuck me. Please."

"Say my name when you ask for it, beautiful."

Scharsi smiled. Tanil still did the bossy thing even after seeing what she was really capable of. The thought faded as quickly as it formed when he climbed up her body and rolled his hips. The action pressed the thick rod of his cock against her swelling clit, sending a shiver from her weeping slit clear up to the base of her skull.

Those glorious hips rolled again. At the same time Tanil nuzzled the downy curls at the nape of her neck. Scharsi gulped in a breath. Let it out on a whoosh. Did it again. It wasn't enough. The man simply overwhelmed her. An unsteady moan worked its way past her frozen throat muscles and made her trachea vibrate.

On a whispered sigh, he said, "Come on, baby. Say it for me."

She knew exactly what he wanted. Before she could help it, the words tumbled out.

"Tan...please. Give it to me."

Holding himself away from her body on his elbows, Tanil looked down at her with a wickedly sensual gleam in his gorgeous dark eyes. Her skin burned where their groins met.

"What exactly do you want?" he growled. "This?" Bending low, his wet, deliciously hot tongue swiped the sensitive skin of her neck muscles up to her ear and then nibbled the little lobe like a sweet treat.

"Or this?" Strong, determined fingers swept underneath the full globe of a breast and weighed the swelling mound. A fingertip and thumb encircled a budding nipple and gently twisted.

"Or…?"

This time the twist was sharper, the pressure heavier.

Gods, how was a girl to choose? She wanted it all.

In between bites and licks, he spoke quietly, the tone so low and deep she felt it in the marrow of her bones. It made her gut dance with a delicious, anxious twitch.

"When you took that guy down, Shar, it turned me on like a fucking switch. It was downright sexy."

"Sexy? Are you high? I broke a man's ribs and it was sexy?"

"Call me demented, but yes. It brought out something primal in me to know that you have all that power, all that strength. Yet you give it to me in the bedroom."

"Half the time I give it. The rest of the time, you take it."

"Yes, but you trust me enough to let me. It means everything, Shar. Now spread those lovely long legs and let me show you what I'm working with."

She laughed, but it quickly became a breathy gasp when Tanil's fingers dipped low and stoked her already flaming pussy.

"You look primed to come again. Think you can give me another one, beautiful?"

"Aaah! Tanil, oh Gods, yes."

He couldn't wait another second to push inside her. The slick dew that met his fingers said she was clearly ready for him. So wet with sweet honey, he drove home in a single, smooth stroke.

"Wrap your legs around me, Shar."

With no hesitation, her lovely thighs pressed against his body just above the waist, holding tight. Ankles crossed as she arched underneath him. Her eyes flew open in surprise when he rolled to bring her on top.

"Stroke yourself while you ride me, beautiful."

Hands planted firmly at her hips, Tanil guided her up and down his aching cock even as his gaze remained glued to the deft fingers attacking her clit. In moments Scharsi was coming again and he was right there with her, tipping headlong into hormone heaven. Ah, endorphins were such lovely things.

The quiet tweep of the entry sensor sounded over their combined panting and happy sighs.

"Who would dare…" Tanil said, knowing his words were barely a growl. What numbskull would bother them now? The whole fucking station had to know what they were doing in here after most of the inhabitants at the market saw him scoop up his woman and land a telling blow on her ass as he carried her off.

It sounded again. Good thing Tanil had thought to lock it since it was obvious that whoever it was had no plans of going away.

Tweeeeep…

Tanil yelled toward the door. "What?!"

"Uh, excuse me. Sorry to interrupt." Wow. It was the voice of one of the men Scharsi had practically stomped a mud hole into. Tanil was shocked the man could talk, let alone make it to their quarters to fetch them. "The Princess and her consorts are waiting for you in Regan's office.

After a two-minute washup, they were quickly back in their clothes and headed out the door. No surprise that their escort wasn't waiting. Too bad. Tanil was curious to see how many different colors Scharsi had turned his face.

Chapter Thirteen

"Okay, here's what we have. I did a bit of hacking into the IMF communications systems through the central servers on Amalgama," Tie informed them.

Scharsi felt her brows crawl up her face in astonishment. How the hell had he done such a thing?

"I used the secured housing unit in Sector Two. I figured I'd get more information from the lower ranks chatter than bothering with the upper asses. Also, those asses figure they don't need much security on the internal systems since the soldiers can only use those channels to talk to each other. And I was right. It seems that the good Captain Tanil's former unit, Kev, is missing."

"What? Missing? But Kev is SS," Tanil said.

"How does a Super Soldier go missing? It's unheard of. No one just drops out of the corps and no one leaves. We escaped, but we're the exceptions, not the rule," Scharsi said.

"True," Tie responded. "But word is that the job to kill Tanil was botched by a SS. This particular missing SS, to be exact."

"Bullshit. SS's don't botch jobs," Regan said.

All of them nodded in agreement. So that meant only one thing. Tanil's jaw clenched in anger as he voiced the length the corps would go through to keep its secret. "It means that Kev didn't intend to kill me. If he had, I'd be dead. Period. But Vulf would know that just as well as we do. He would have concluded that Kev defied his orders. Then Kev gets "disappeared" or Vulf risks the SS being questioned by his handlers. The SS wouldn't hesitate to reveal his actions to his handler. After all, he couldn't be punished for carrying out a kill order, 'cause an order is an order is an order. Follow it, or else."

Scharsi added, "But Vulf is a different story. Even he wouldn't be exempt from punishment for ordering the assassination of a fellow Amalgamation officer."

"Former Amalgamation officer, thank you very much," Tanil said.

"Right." Regan smiled. It was a scary thing to behold, that smile.

"I'm not sure I understand this handler-to-soldier relationship," Cerise questioned, her pretty brow scrunched into a frown.

"Vulf can give orders to the units under his

command, but he can't order them to keep whatever they see or hear from their handlers. The handlers have the real control, the real authority. Super Soldiers know that much better than the fucktards like Vulf do. It's pounded into them each and every day." Scharsi said.

"And contrary to the myths perpetrated by the feds, Super Soldiers aren't walking zombies with no minds of their own. They aren't stupid."

"Why thank you, Tanil dear," Tie said sarcastically. Cerise laughed outright. The sound was infectious even as Tie batted his lashes at Tanil with a genuine twinkle in his opaque grayish-whites that declared his modified genes.

After getting her giggling under control, Cerise leaned into Tie and said, "Give them the last, babe." Tie looked up at the little princess as if she hung the moons. Then again, to this particular male, perhaps she hung every moon in this quadrant.

For a moment, Scharsi was distracted at her own happiness — happiness that she'd found love and that her fellow SS had too. What were the odds?

"And last, we have information from some of our contacts that strange, even unknown illnesses have been reported in some of the resistance camps. Thankfully none of those who'd gotten ill were high up enough on the food chain to spill much to their Amalgamation "doctors". They did notice, however, that the doctors were awful tightlipped in telling them what they had. Gave 'em shots that hurt like hell, though."

"So, where are we going? What's the plan?" Scharsi asked point-blank.

"Tell us what you think is the best way to go," Tie said. "After all, you're the one trained for analytics and reasoning. It only makes sense that you would come up with what makes the most sense, then let us work up the logistics on how to make it happen. While my specialty is computers and technology, I really just like to blow shit up."

Regan slipped an arm around Tie and said, "Well that makes two of us."

"Three of us, baby," Cerise chimed in.

Regan's lips spread with a grin that made Tanil's stomach dance and the skin over his spine dampen with a cold sweat. He sent up a silent prayer.

Dear Gods, thank you that these people are on our side, otherwise I'd be shitting in my pants just now. Amen.

He couldn't help but wince as he rubbed the spot where a crater from Kev's laser pistol used to be. Nor, even in the levity of the moment, could he suppress the grief that welled up in his soul to know that someone, Kev, had knowingly given his life for him.

Epilogue

With a comm tab pressed discreetly behind her ear, Scharsi confirmed her position. They'd decided she would have the best chance of getting in and out of the so-called secure hotel where Vulf was vacationing on Chalis Prime. Dressed like one of the maintenance crew, she'd simply walked in the back door and flashed the forged entry badge that Tie had made for her across the entry sensor. Tie really was a whiz. He'd accessed the personnel records of the cleanup crew assigned to the wing where Vulf had rooms, then downloaded their personal information, including bioscans. With that information he'd created Scharsi a whole new persona wrapped in a two millimeter thick plastic card. And since the staff security was all automated, there was no flesh and blood person on duty at that hour to bust her like there was at the front of the building.

This was the city of Beyer San, a metropolitan sprawl with skyscrapers of synthsteel and glass-like panes. There were high-rise living spaces and plenty of places to dine and party for those who lived, worked and played here. But it was also a prime location for the creation of medicines, both legal and otherwise. And this particular building sat on top of an underground lab where black market biotech compounds were made.

And if Tie was able to get that bit of information to Scharsi, that meant Vulf knew as well, considering this would be the ideal place to have something made that wasn't supposed to exist. Ever.

And Vulf was a pompous ass. What person with common sense would open the door to the maintenance crew at two in the morning with the claim of a chemical emergency? Idiot. These were black market drugs, which meant if something went wrong during the manufacturing process there would certainly be no alarms.

Ever grateful for the man's stupidity, Scharsi was in and out in ten minutes, which meant Tanil hadn't needed to run to the rescue or blow anything up.

And now, after confirming her location with Tanil, Scharsi and her quarry cleared the brightly lit strip and headed out to a more industrial area. The perfect place for a couple of private landing pads and a dozen or so empty hangars.

Mere minutes after she and Tanil were off-planet, a too-sexy hail sounded through the con.

"Hello, beautiful. Are you ready for me?"

Tanil rolled his eyes. Scharsi laughed.

"Hi, Sealy. Docking clamps in place and the hatch is unlocked. Come on over."

"Is the prisoner still unconscious?"

"Yep. He'll give you no trouble, though he is a bit of dead weight. The sed will wear off in about six hours."

"You sure you don't want to just blow him out the airlock instead?" Tan suggested.

"For once, I'm with Tannie," Sealy said.

"I'd rather him spend some time in the Abyss in The Devil's Pit. I'm sure Vulf will enjoy answering a few questions from anyone who cares to ask while he waits on someone to come and claim him."

"But as the person who placed the bounty on Vulf, you would have to be the one to release him into the custody of the Amalgamation so he can stand trial."

"Oh, I'm aware of that. Guess he'll be waiting awhile. I'm suddenly so busy with my new BHI job I just can't find the time to fetch the asshole anytime soon."

"Damn, beautiful," Sealy crooned, "remind me never to piss you off."

With a chuckle, she said, "Computer, release lower-level hatch."

"Yes, Commander."

With Vulf on his way to spend some time at The Devil's Pit, Scharsi considered just relaxing a bit. After all, she'd not only brought Carl's killer to justice, but Tanil's attempted murderer as well. She should have been satisfied, but wasn't surprised when she found she wasn't.

It was time to put the next part of their plan into action.

She turned to Tanil and caught the same determination in his eyes that mirrored the one in her soul.

"Time to plant more seeds of rebellion, Tanil. Put the rumor out that the Amalgamation is both killing and infecting its own to keep its misdeeds from getting out."

"Works for me, beautiful. Let's go make

some new enemies."

With a smile as bright as the Trevosian Blue Sun, Scharsi said, "Better yet, let's just piss off the old ones."

Glossary

Aboolan: The natural inhabitants of the Aboo System and its planets who moved on after beings from Earth moved in to mine the planets for their natural resources.

Aboo System: Home of the Aboo mining planets. Crystolium-rich planets located two Smith Gates from Earth.

Aboo Two: Second planet in the Aboo System where Amalgama, the capital city of the Amalgamation of Planets, is located.

Aboolan War of 2112: War that broke out when Earthlings invaded the Aboo System for the planets' natural resources.

Abyss, The: Section of The Web where prisoners are kept until transported to another planet or prison facility.

Amalgama: The capital city and chief headquarters for the Amalgamation of Planets. A large, dome-covered city located on the planet Aboo Two.

Amalgamation of Planets: The primary governing body of the galaxy.

Amaya: Cintealios capital city on the planet of the same name.

Aurelie: The Web's day shift cook.

Azo Eta: Planet very similar to Earth, located in the Secundus System.

Bounty-hunter class: Class of small ships, specially suited to carry and operate with only a small crew. Preferred mode of transportation of the bounty hunters, hence the name.

Bounty Hunters, Inc.: Organization of bounty hunters set up and run by Ulric Vonner. They work for large fees and at their own discretion and are neither good nor bad, though they will break the law when necessary in order to bring in a bounty.

Bulkhead Disrupting Charge: Fired from a normal missile cannon, the charge attaches itself to a target's shields, weakens the shields, opens a hole through the target's defenses and fires a concentrated charge into the target's hull. Inflicts major, concentrated damage to a ship's hull.

Cintealios: The warrior race. These beings are human/humanoid and live to conquer those who are weaker. Largest opposing force to the Amalgamation.

Comm-tabs: Buttonlike communication devices that are pressed to the skin behind the ear.

Constance O'Rourke: Supply handler for The Web.

Control: Small space station situated near the Smith Gate. Controls the energy field that operates the gates and determines where a ship will emerge from the wormhole.

Copper Arrow: Copper balls that expand into shafts of corresponding light; an arrow that explodes on contact.

Devil's Pit: Seedy neighborhood on Quartus Seven where The Web is located. Location chosen specifically for its rough appearance and dangerous atmosphere.

Dexter Smith: "Dex", The Web's computer geek. If it's electronic, he can figure it out.

"Doc": Holographic doctor in The Web's medical wing. He has numerous robotic shells that he can download himself into, to perform various functions.

Executioner: Ulric Vonner's personal bounty-class cruiser.

Gold Arrow: Gold balls that expand into shafts of corresponding light and act as a claw, anchoring target to whatever solid surface is behind it, such as a wall.

Halcion Cartiere: Top commanding officer of the Interplanetary Military Forces.

Hub: The heart of The Web, located at the very center. Also contains the Conference Room where meetings are held.

Hunter Pack: Small backpack that holds more than it appears to hold.

Icsantheze Dagger: Daggers created on the planet Icsanthia. Sixty-six centimeters total length from tip of the dagger blade to the end of the handle—fifteen-centimeter hilt, fifty-one centimeter blade. The blade is curved like a serpent slithering across a surface, golden in color, with pale green streaks through the blade. Handle is wrapped in emerald leather.

Interplanetary Military Forces (IMF): The military power behind the Amalgamation that works diligently to protect the Amalgamation and everything it stands for.

Intergalactic Security Agency (ISA): The job of the ISA is to explore new worlds and collect critical intelligence on any alien species discovered.

Interplanetary Senate: Body of five hundred representatives from across the galaxy. Most major systems are represented in the Senate—

five representatives each — with a few exceptions.

Jacobi Smith (deceased): Discovered wormholes usable for faster travel times. The wormholes became known as Smith Gates in his honor.

Jiborui: Home world of Krys Xan, the Amalgamation of Planets' leader. Exotic planet that is home to humanoid, hermaphrodite beings who are tall and slender, and have very sharp minds. Key in the production of many space travel inventions that have made traveling throughout the galaxy and colonizing new worlds easier.

Jump Drives: Allows the vessel to navigate through nearby wormholes, effectively reducing travel times significantly. (Note: Control must open the gate. Also controls to which neighboring system the gate connects.)

Krys Xan: Hermaphrodite from Jurgia and leader of the Amalgamation of Planets. He presides over the Senate and all its members.

Military Sciences Lab: Based on Earth, its purpose is to create and cultivate the ultimate soldier.

Nursotics: Robotic nurses.

Orbit Wisps: Spectral, universal snitches.

They barter information for energy cubes.

PHD: Personal Holographic Device. When activated, it alters the hunter's appearance, aiding in acquiring a bounty.

Plasma Cannons: Can target an enemy ship's deflector shield and will drain the energy from the shield determinant to the size of the charge. If used on a small ship without a shield, it can slowly deteriorate the ship's hull.

Quartus Seven: Planet where The Web is located. Also known as The City Planet. Seventy-five percent of the planet's surface is covered by one continuous metropolitan area. The remaining twenty-five percent of the planet is covered in water. No indigenous life forms or plant life exist here.

Replicators: Basic replication of items such as food and clothing. Complex machinery cannot be replicated, though the replicator can retrieve items from storage compartments.

Sa-Ro Five: Largest agricultural hub in the Secundus System. This planet supplies food rations to many planets, including some from neighboring systems.

Scanners: Allow the ship's crew to scan other ships, space stations or planets for signs of life.

Sealy Garrison: Constance O'Rourke's assistant. If Constance isn't available, Sealy is the man to see.

Secret Sciences Police (SSP): Formed to ensure that no one toys with time travel or biowar sciences, to protect the Amalgamation and its interests.

Secundus System: System to which Quartus Seven belongs. Similar to Earth's system, Secundus possesses nine planets, many of which are uninhabitable due to extreme atmospheric conditions, though the use of atmospheric domes enables limited habitation of some of the planets.

Silver Arrow: Silver balls that expand into shafts of corresponding light and only work as a piercing weapon.

Smith Gate: Device used to access wormholes. It is located near the largest, most advanced planet in the system and significantly cuts down travel times.

Smith Hole: Proper name for the wormholes used by Smith Gates.

Spectra-shades: Special shades used to see Orbit Wisps.

Super Soldiers: Bio-engineered super soldiers, produced on Earth as supreme fighting beings.

The Web: Base of operations for Bounty Hunters, Inc.

Tomozava: A blue fleshy vegetable that is a cross between a tomato and a zava vegetable.

Tranq-ring: Ring that administers a dose of tranquilizer to a bounty/person/being but does not affect the ring's wearer.

T-Sdei Delta: The party planet. Located in the Secundus System, neighboring Quartus Seven.

Ulric Vonner: President and founder of Bounty Hunters, Inc.

Vanquiguard: Wristband that, when activated, creates an energy shield to protect the wearer.

Zava: Blue, tomato-like vegetable that is indigenous to the planet Azo Eta. Also known as tomozava.

Zeri: Night shift cook for The Web.

CONTINUE READING
to enjoy a sneak peek at chapters from
Wind and Fire, Gathering of the Storms
Volume I
by T.J. Michaels

Wind and Fire
Gathering of the Storms Book One
Volume One

by

T.J. Michaels

Chapter One

"Grandfather, if you must summon me from my pleasant dreams you could at least fashion a place more interesting," RuArk said softly into the darkness.

The room was stark, dimly lit, and completely empty — no windows, no doors. RuArk leaned against a rough wall with one foot propped up behind him, arms crossed over his chest. He smiled at the image of his favorite relative — an Elder known to all their clan as the Grandfather.

RuArk's brow furrowed as he watched the ethereal essence of the Grandfather's body shift and shimmer. Strange. It was as if he had difficulty staying with RuArk in a place where all was typically at the Elder's command. The Dream was a place where one was not confined to the body; able to move through time and space with¬out the inhibition of flesh and bone. There was nothing to fear, though things appeared vividly real. It was one of several places to seek wisdom and direction, or face your greatest challenges. As he gazed at the roiling image, he noted the deep frown marring the old man's ancient features.

When he finally spoke, the Grandfather's urgency-laced words formed as ice in the pit of RuArk's stomach. Gifts lost to all, except the Gaian, since the Breaking of the world gave protection to the wielder. Those without were vulnerable in this place. If they lost their way, their physical body remained in a state of deep sleep until they either managed to escape or someone guided them out. Unseen forces ruled this realm, and not all were friendly.

"The High Counsel of Draema sought us out in the Dream. Alone."

"Why would he do such a thing? He knows the risks better than anyone."

"He searched for your father to ask for your help," said the Grandfather. "Thank gods it was I who found him as he wandered."

"But why didn't he just come to me directly? I departed the High City not more than three days past. Negotiations were completed, and I am on my way home."

"Not any longer. You must return. This danger is focused on his daughter."

The coldness in RuArk's gut transformed into a 'berg, though it should be no surprise to learn 'that' particular female — Rhia

Greysomne—was in trouble. He hadn't seen her while he'd been in the High City this time. In fact, he hadn't seen her on any of his journeys to Draema Proper over the years. Though he hadn't sought her out, surely he would have heard of any threat to her?

RuArk tensed and pushed away from the wall. "Focused on Rhia? By who?"

"The High Counsel believes one of his own is responsible. He is wise enough to accept that he needs someone outside of his own province. Now, I have told you all I can. You will have to find the rest of your answers in the *Seeking*, and quickly."

The urgent energy that rolled off the Elder's image spiked.

"What aren't you telling me, Elder?"

The Grandfather usually epitomized calm…but not today. His anger-infused growl was cut off with a thick, veil-like silence as he took an uncharacteristic moment to gather himself. Not good.

Finally, he ground out, "There is a taint, a strange darkness in the otherrealms. When the Realmwalkers first noticed, it was quite subtle. Now it seems to have found a focus. It grows bolder, and nearer to the High Counsel's daughter. If you are not in the appointed place at the appointed time, the bringer of this taint will prevail."

"Prevail over what, Grandfather? Over who?"

"I cannot say. It is no longer safe here, even for our kind. But know that I have faith in you, akicita. As such, your Gift of Vision will not fail you."

RuArk's head tilted a hard left.

What Gift of Vision?

The ability to enter the Dream or go on a *Seeking* quest didn't count as a Gift considering any Gaian could do it. But the Gift of Vision? That was something different. In fact, RuArk had never manifested such a Gift. Or any Gift for that matter. While some of his kin had been late bloomers in this regard, RuArk's bud had been on the tree so long, surely it had dried up and fallen off by now. He opened his mouth to ask.

With a warm smile and twinkling dark eyes that crinkled in the corners, the shifting misty presence of The Grandfather shattered before snapping whole once again.

"Go. I will get word to the High Counsel to expect your return to the High City. I will guard over Rhia as best I can until then."

The Elder's shimmering image lost the battle of holding its form and winked out just as RuArk was tossed headlong out of the Dream and slammed back into his own body.

* * * * *

Rama Collaidh sat in his official offices. His fingertips itched to roam over the smooth desktop, to trace the rare veins of gray and silver threaded throughout the polished, white stone. At well past midnight, the window coverings were locked down tight. The dimmed iozene lamp over his workspace gave off the only light in the room. He liked the darkness. It offered a sense of comfort, sitting there surrounded by shadows.

Carefully laid plans were flipped back and forth in his mind — turned sideways and upside down in his mind as he examined them for any holes. Many of his fellow Council members considered him an ambitious, middle-aged nuisance. He could care less what his peers thought. He was in the prime of his life; wily and determined enough to achieve the impossible. And he had the High Counsel's ear.

Yes, his board was set and the pieces were

finally moving. Just as he noted a possible strategic problem, gooseflesh plumped just under the surface of his skin from scalp to fingertips. Sweat beaded between his shoulder blades before slipping coldly down his spine. In spite of the urge to shudder, Collaidh forced his stylus to move smoothly over the viewer embedded in the top of his desk.

He didn't bother to turn towards the source of his discomfort. There was only one person, one thing, that could make him break out in a cold sweat. Could enter his offices unseen. How long had the creature been standing there watching? Collaidh quickly dismissed the concern. His determination to have what he wanted was stronger than fear or foe.

"So, you've finally come," Collaidh muttered.

The words hung in the gloom for what seemed like eons.

"You summoned me, did you not?" The tone was flat, uncaring, and alarmingly similar to his own.

"Have you succeeded in reaching Rhia Greysomne?" Collaidh asked coldly.

Now the deep, silky voice took on a harsh edge of impatience. "Someone is protecting her now, warding her while she sleeps. I cannot summon her into the Dream at all. Yet before the warding began…"

"Get to the point, Behn. And step out where I can see you, damn it."

Collaidh forced himself to look directly into the white eyes of the thing's too-pale face. The only true color on the creature was its clothing. Even the thick, billowing tresses of his shoulder-length hair were white as full moonlight. Everything about him was unnatural. Yet for all that, how did he manage to be so bloody handsome?

Once he was fully into what little light there was, Behn smiled.

The grin chilled the blood. Collaidh's lip curled at the sight of gleaming, elongated incisors—longer than any normal man's. And slightly yellowed.

Must be from endless cycles of feeding.

The thought turned his stomach.

Yes, Behn spoke with sophisticated diction, but he was far from civilized. And only a fool would forget it.

"When asleep," Behn said, "a person without the Gifts is vulnerable once inside the Dream. Strangely, Rhia does not have this vulnerability. The most I could do was deliver the most fantastic nightmares. I believe I was slowly wearing her down, though I could not directly manipulate her."

"So what. Get to the point."

"We have encountered a problem. I am unable to touch her dreams at all now. She is either Gifted, or someone with the Gifts is protecting her."

"That's impossible!" Collaidh shot to his feet. Palm slammed against the sturdy desk hard enough to sting. "Her father is the High Counsel. The man is Draeman, through and through."

"What of her mother? Rhia is half-Gaian, is she not? Perhaps the mother has passed on a Gift?" Behn insisted calmly.

Collaidh frowned. Hell. He hadn't thought of that. Hadn't anticipated any of these delays. But he had to keep the upper hand. Behn had proven to be keenly intelligent, single-minded and ruthlessly ambitious — a creature that would take advantage of any perceived weakness. No one could know he'd enlisted the aid of a creature that shouldn't exist — one that had rediscovered how to manipulate magick long lost…

But then, who would believe it? After all,

this was Draema Province. Science ruled all.

With a smile that felt venomous even to himself, Collaidh pushed the thoughts away, deciding to force his point with his unwelcome, but much needed visitor.

"Look, the only people with Gifts are Gaian. Rhia's mother was, and remains, the only Gaian woman to marry outside her province since who knows how long. The woman is long dead, and certainly not around to teach her daughter anything about Gaia, Gifts, or anything else. And we all know the High Counsel hasn't tried in the least to teach Rhia anything about her mother's people since the girl was eight years old. Perhaps you're simply not capable of getting the job done?"

"Careful, old man."

Behn's feral growl sent Collaidh's heart into a stutter, but he was unwilling to give any ground. Collaidh ground his back teeth. This was his show to run, damn it. No way would he allow Behn to take control. He painted his face with a calm façade and refused to look away from the gleaming, white eyes. Eyes that seemed to bore right through his forehead.

"I said forget the High Counsel. We need that woman. We need Rhia, period." Settling back again into the plush cushions of his chair, Collaidh turned and unlocked a small drawer. "Perhaps this will help," he said as he held out a small amber vial filled with a milky looking fluid.

Collaidh steeled himself as perfectly manicured, long, semi-translucent fingers reached toward him. Little blue veins made various patterns underneath the smooth white skin. It made Collaidh's skin crawl when the lukewarm fingers touched his palm to retrieve the vial.

"What is this?" Behn asked.

"Don't worry about what it is. I called in a favor from a friend in the Society of Physicians. It won't harm her. Since the Dream business is no longer an option, you'll need to be more direct. This will make Rhia more cooperative."

"Fine. I will deliver it to someone who can get close to her. It must be done discretely if we are to avoid suspicion."

"I agree. You can't be seen here," Collaidh sniffed.

"If there is one thing I am good at, it is concealing myself from friends and enemies alike. And if I choose to be seen, I will simply be mistaken for my brother, would I not?

The sneer in Behn's voice was unmistakable. Collaidh grimaced at the bitterness in those words. Was it justified? Definitely. But he couldn't afford to be moved by it. Not now. Not ever.

"Perhaps," Collaidh responded, but didn't think it possible that Behn would ever be mistaken for his brother—a man who looked fully human, while it was obvious that Behn was…not. "But don't take any chances. I don't want anyone to become aware of your presence here. Besides, those teeth and eyes of yours would give you away for sure. You'd be shot on sight. What good would you be to me then? Unfortunately we need each other so let's make the best of it, shall we?"

"You promised to give Rhia to me. You will keep your promise, old man."

"Yes, yes, yes," Collaidh said, waving his hand dismissively. "I said you could have her once she's served my purpose. Now leave me alone. I have work to do."

Collaidh turned his back and ignored the wave of anger emanating from behind him. He didn't hear Behn leave, but was vastly relieved when the little hairs on the back of his neck finally stopped dancing.

* * * * *

Sara rose and donned a warm fluffy robe. She crossed the dark room to turn up the delicate-looking iozene sconces mounted on the walls. As she reached out her hand to adjust the brightness, her skin went cold. She was no longer alone. He was here. She expected no greeting and received none. He didn't care for niceties, only obedience.

"You will put this in the First Heir's teapot this morning. Do you understand?"

"I understand." Sara replied softly, her head tilted down in a genuinely terrified posture. "But her companion brings her breakfast in the mornings. How am I supposed to do this?" she asked on a shaky whisper.

"You will find a way, Sara."

She nodded quickly as he gave instruction and pressed a small glass vial into the center of her sweaty palm.

"Do you want to know what it is, sweet Sara?"

"N-No, sir. No, I don't." Sara clutched the vial firmly against her breast. Knowing too much simply wasn't a good thing with this man.

He moved closer, his long, dark coat swished against her bare ankles as he shifted behind her. His breath was both warm and cool against the nape of her neck. Darkness radiated from him.

She shivered uncontrollably.

"Good girl, Sara. Very good indeed," he crooned against her skin as his fingers skimmed lightly over her shoulders. Her mind said she should run screaming from this creature, but her body wanted him—wanted to feel the thick mass of snow-white hair slide over her skin. To feel his teeth scrape against her shoulder as he took her roughly. Her sex warmed and softened in need of the thick erection pressed against her backside. Ashamed, Sara closed her eyes against her physical reaction to such an unnatural man. When she opened them again, she was in bed.

Blinking into the darkness, a wave of relief swept over her. It was a dream. It always seemed so real. Even the sensitive buds of her nipples puckered at the false memory of his breath wafting over her skin. She rose, wrapped her robe closely about her body, and went through the motions she could have sworn she'd already done. Slipping her hands into the warm pockets, Sara went dead still when her fingers wrapped around a small glass vial.

"How in blazes does he do that?" She almost wished she had the courage to ask him. Almost.

She washed up quickly. Dressed in her Houseman's uniform, she slipped the vial into her trouser pocket. As she rushed to the kitchens, Sara pushed away guilt for what she was about to do. Failure equaled pain—lots and lots of brilliantly delivered pain—courtesy of a much too-handsome devil that was supposed to exist only in dreams. Unfortunately for her, he didn't seem inclined to stay there.

Chapter Two

By the time Rhia made it to the dining hall, she looked and felt like every description of hell she'd ever read about in the old story books. In addition to the sweat and dirt stains that covered her tunic, her leggings sported a long, jagged rip. The fabric flapped annoyingly as she walked, baring a good amount of thigh. She'd almost had her leg sliced open in the middle of teaching the final knife-fighting session of the day. Good thing she hadn't been instructing laser whips instead. Geesh.

She pushed the thoughts away, and instead focused on what awaited her upstairs in her rooms—a blasted bath, and she couldn't wait to sink into the warm…ewww!

She sniffed and then sniffed again. Was that rank smell her, or the filleted protein on her plate? Not wanting to offend, Rhia ate quickly at a table closest to the wide double doors and headed up to her apartments.

The twitchy burn in her legs made her hiss out loud as she climbed the tower stairs. Wiped out, and absolutely tired of being so damn tired, she forced herself to trudge on. Why did her place have to be on the only floor that couldn't be accessed by a lift?

Finally at the top of the tower stairs, she reached for the key around her neck. Her hand brushed the sharp corner of a note she'd completely forgotten about. Removing the crumpled piece of paper from her breast pocket, Rhia immediately recognized her father's bold, flowing script. Even bolder words had her bristling before she was halfway through the short missive.

To: Rhia Greysomne, First Heir to the Seven Colonies of Draema Province

Consider this a formal reprimand from the Office of the High Counsel. I don't have time to run all over the City looking for you as you take on more and more responsibilities. I had to send a Houseman to find you to deliver this note. I'm sure he's just catching up with you and it's probably well past dinner time as you're reading it.

"Damn it, how does he always know?" she wondered aloud.

You are hereby relieved of all duties except for the diplomatic responsibilities of the First Heir. In addition, you may teach one, and only

one, combat or blade class. All of your other
duties related to the Society of War have been
assigned to other officers. Further, you are to
leave at first light for Harbor Station to inspect
the two new airships built for the coastal patrols.
You will also inspect the troops stationed there
under your brother's command. Joan Rouillard
and Brita Shae will accompany you. To make the
journey shorter, I've assigned you a hover
driver. He'll take you to the train, where you'll
board for Harbor Station. And no, you may not
take the outmoded form of transportation you
prefer — that damned horse of yours.

It was bad enough he was making her take
the train to the harbors, but she wouldn't be
allowed to even transport herself to the station?
Not that she knew how to operate one of the
hover things anyway, but that wasn't the point.
And Moonlight was not outmoded, damn it!

With an annoyed huff, she finished reading.

I advise you to find time to enjoy yourself
while you are at Harbor Station, young lady.
You will come to my offices before you leave to
pick up a message for your brother. When you
return to the High City, your life will change
considerably.

Regards,

Grey Greysomne, High Counsel of Draema Province

Commander in Chief, Society of War

Her father had sent a note to tell her off. This was a new experience. Grey Greysomne usually delivered any displeasure directly to her face. But a note? Geez, how impersonal could you get? And what did he mean her life would 'change considerably' when she returned from Harbor Station? And why did she need to go inspect a ship or troops? Her younger brother was the Harbormaster for a reason. That man knew all there was to know about the blasted vessels. What a total waste of time. But as one of the highest-ranking officers of the Society of War, she had her orders and would obey them. Of course she wouldn't admit to being secretly pleased with the opportunity to visit her brother and his family. Perhaps she'd rest better there.

Rhia cringed as she recalled the weeks of nightmares so terrifying, so wrong, that she'd jerked herself awake with a scream on her lips. There'd been several nights where she'd awoken with sweat-soaked bed linens stuck to her body as she sat huddled in the center of the bed. She was sure her skin had tried to crawl away and hide a time or two.

But last night everything had changed. Sleep had been peaceful and strangely calm with the presence of an old man. Her dream had been simple—the man seemed to enjoy nothing more than keeping her company, and the nasties had stayed away. It would be nice to drift off and not wonder what was in store. Maybe some rest and a change of scenery would do just that. Perhaps Harbor Station was the ticket.

Rhia read the note again, stuffed it back into her pocket, and fumbled with her key tag. The flat, square fob gleamed dully in the bluish light of the iozene lamps set into the walls. Holding the tag to the center of the panel next to the door, a familiar click indicated the release of the lock.

One step into her private domain, Rhia felt the cares of the day melt away. This space was uniquely hers. It was strategically unsound to have walls an enemy could hide behind, so there were none in this space. Instead, it was large, airy, and tastefully arranged so she could see from one end of the suite to the other without obstruction.

The sleeping area was dominated by a huge, curtained bed, but it was the floor that defined the space. It was covered with soft, gray, hand-knotted carpets. Where the carpets ended, so did her sleeping area. A large mosaic of tiny gray and white tiles in the shape of the sigil of the House of Greysomne covered the dining area floor. It was centered by a large table; its base of polished marble was topped with a thick, smoky glass pane. Off to the left was the mantel covered with awards and weapons, over a wide, and thankfully blazing, iozene fireplace.

A few steps past her large, four-post bed, a chilly wind sent the silky bed curtains billowing. The mid-winter breeze flowed through the glass doors that led to her private balcony... Only she was sure those doors were closed and locked this morning. Brita would have been the last person out of these rooms, and she would never have left them unsecured.

Shivering from the whoosh of cool air, Rhia dropped her blade and belt down on top of the dining table with a loud clunk as she passed. She pressed the little switches that controlled the wall of thick, beveled panes and waited impatiently as the glass slid silently along the tracks.

The moment the balcony doors closed, her trouble meter tipped off the scale. Turning ever so slowly, she peered into the darkness. Sharp senses tried to see and hear everything at once as her eyes adjusted.

The open curtains let in the glow of a half-moon, whose light was obscured by a passing cloud. Looking past the mantle, Rhia peered toward the bathroom entrance. The sheer curtains that gave her privacy were pulled open as usual.

However, what was unusual was the shadowed figure standing there. A black cloak swirled around a body as it took a step forward, and the "it" was revealed as a man.

"Hello, Rhia."

Bryan Collaidh? Aw hell. She hadn't seen him since she'd made First Blade, cycles ago. The haunted look on his face, and the dark shadows under his eyes, made it obvious those cycles had not been kind. His pale skin stood out in stark contrast against lackluster, shoulder-length black hair. Didn't he know greasy hair was out of style in Draema? And what was with the all-black garb?

The creep hadn't left the province under the best of circumstances. As far as she was concerned, he was still unwelcome in the High City, and certainly unwelcome in her personal space.

"What the hell are you doing here?" she

asked, not bothering to hide the contempt in her voice.

The lines of his mouth hinted at the cruelty she knew he was capable of. A malevolent black gaze followed her steps. Deep set, and round as old-fashioned playing stones, his eyes seemed too large for his face. He looked like an overgrown guppy, complete with thin, pouting lips. An image popped into her head of this unwanted guest, complete with gills and fins. His lips glub-glub-glubbed as bubbles floated up towards the surface of the river she wanted to drown him in.

Her amusement faded quickly as she considered the situation. It took a bold man to break into her apartments with no fear. Why would he take such a risk? The answer was obvious—he still didn't have any goddamn common sense.

Rhia watched him closely as she walked across the room. The glowing fireplace halfway between them cast his smooth, black clothing with an eerie, orange tint.

"I asked what you're doing here, Bryan." At the mantle now, she stretched her hands toward the warming flames, appearing completely at ease.

"I've come to visit you, old friend," he drawled, moving slowly toward her. He attempted to smile, but it must have made his face hurt. The skin appeared to freeze just around his mouth in the middle of the feeble attempt.

"Old friend? What are you, nuts? I haven't seen you since the day you decided to use my face as a punching bag."

"I'm a changed man, Rhia. Cycles of surviving on the borders can do that to a person." He ground out the words as his gaze seemed to focus on something far, far away. Some called the borders "Hell's Eastern Seventh Level." Judging from the menace rolling off of her nemesis, like dust clouds of choking malintent, the name must be pretty accurate.

She took a deep breath, then another. Blast it, she'd always been calm when meeting a foe. But she'd never faced a known enemy whose very presence dragged one of the worst moments of her life out of the locked dungeon of her mind.

But her typical pre-fight calm was nowhere to be found. No, she was torqued the hell off. And this wasn't going to end nicely.

She almost smiled.

Biding her time, Rhia leaned against the smooth mantle with one arm draped casually atop the ledge. Her fingertips brushed the hilt of the specially commissioned blade her father had given her on her sixteenth birthday. For a few seconds she considered pulling the razor sharp work of art down off the mounting, but changed her mind. The blade was too special to dirty on the likes of Bryan Collaidh. Too bad she didn't have a laser pistol handy. At least those left wounds that didn't bleed much. Rhia was sharp enough to know that this little conversation was going to end in a fight, and the less blood on her tile, the better. She hated cleaning blood out of crystal grout.

Then she noticed that Bryan wasn't moving. Simply stood there, wasting her time.

"Look Bryan, I'm tired. I had a long day, and I really don't feel like being bothered. I was so busy this evening I was two hours late to dinner. Now I'm two hours late for bed. Can't you just go away? Perhaps we can talk in the morning." Knowing she didn't mean a word of that last part. After all, there was nothing to say.

"You have grown into a beautiful woman, Rhia. And I think I'd rather talk now. Besides, I've returned to Draema Proper for one purpose.

To claim you."

Laughter bubbled up out of her throat before she could stop it. She just couldn't help it. Claim her? Ridiculous! Her smile was genuine, but her thoughts took another turn, and her insides turned with it. What if he was serious? A serious lunatic, that is. He wanted her? Why? He certainly didn't love her. She didn't think he even liked her.

Sigh.

Okay, he had about an inch on her in height, and maybe twenty pounds in weight. The calculations only took a moment. She could take him down fast, then call in a favor to a couple of the soldiers who roomed on the floors below. The advantage of living in her father's Citadel – it only took seconds to get someone up here to help drag the body away.

But Bryan still hadn't moved. Not even to blink. Perhaps a reminder that she outranked him would push him over the edge so they could get this over with.

She rolled her eyes and said sleepily, "Get out, you idiot. Otherwise, as the highest ranking officer in the Society of War, I'll personally have you assigned to the iozene mines with all the other miscreants."

Then she waited for him to lose it like he had long ago, when he'd taken a closed fist to her face. Her offense—a rank promotion ahead of him. Angry and full of jealousy, he used his failure as an excuse to abuse her. In his mind, the anger had been all her fault. Personal responsibility? Puh. Those two words weren't in his vocabulary.

Hands raised in surrender, he headed toward the door. Halfway there, he changed direction.

Damn it.

He looked back and forth, between her and the katana lying on the table. The metal under the black leather, which crisscrossed elegantly over the handle, gleamed dully in the moonlight. Bryan picked it up, testing the weight of it in his hand.

Calculation flared in those cold, black eyes as he took a single step, pivoted and threw the weapon clear across the room. It bounced off a wall near the front door with a loud clang. She had no doubts now—the man was definitely nuts.

From rage to cool civility in a blink, he crooned, "I hear you've made Blademaster well before the usual ten cycles. But it doesn't matter whether you're a Blademaster or not, we're going to reinstate our former engagement."

Bullshit.

One hand on her hip, she took an angry step forward. "My father didn't approve of you back then, and he certainly won't approve now. Besides, if you were on the up-and-up, you wouldn't have broken in and waited for me in the dark. What the hell do you really want?"

"Give me a minute. I'm sure you'll figure it out." He lunged.

* * * * *

Rhia was ready, and ducked past him so fast he found himself facing the fireplace with nothing but air where she had been seconds before. A clean kick to his kidneys from behind slammed him chest-first into the mantle. The wind whooshed from his lungs. After a few wheezing breaths, he faced her with eyes drawn tight in an angry frown. And a bit of…shock?

"Surprise, asshole."

He hadn't expected her to be able to defend herself without a weapon. Well good. But she'd rather have a blade between them. Rhia ran for her steel.

Bryan dove, taking her feet out from under her. She went down hard, skinning her cheek on the smooth, hard mosaic under the dining table. But stinging cheeks were a relief. If she'd landed a few more inches to the left, her jaw would have made solid contact with the glass and marble of the table.

She rolled over with a groan and was happy to be in absolute pain rather than knocked out cold.

Then he was on her, trying to capture her hands as they connected with his eyes, cheeks, and lips. Rage, thick and palpable filled the bit of air between them.

"I'll have what I want whether you agree or not, Rhia." Pant. "Once I fuck you." Snarl. "I'll present evidence to the Council."

What the hell?

"Your honor," he sneered as if she had none, "will require you to declare me your mate. Our houses will be joined one way or another. Good thing you were altered at the Age of Consent. Without a hymen, at least it won't hurt. Much."

Whoa. How did he know when she'd been altered? And what the hell else did he know? The records of every member of the Society of War, especially hers as First Heir, were classified. No one knew her secret other than her father, and her friends, Brita and Joan.

Her mind screeched to a halt. The law was clear. As female First Heir, she'd had her hymen painlessly removed at the Age of Consent as required. But afterward, Rhia didn't have the Draeman privilege of screwing around.

While mates, lovers and Sensuan were carefully recorded for all members of the Society of War, for Rhia the rules were a bit different. She had two choices — she could take an assigned lover for a time, whose identity and time of service were carefully determined and recorded.

Or she could take a mate. Period.

Her mate's identity would remain secret for a time until she declared the union to the Council, or proof of consummation was given. Vows could be taken in the presence of her father and a witness, or she could elope. This was to keep the First Heir's mate from being assassinated before he could actually say, "I do."

No one, especially Bryan Collaidh, should know that her records were clean – no assigned lover, no mate. If he managed to prove he'd had sex with her, she was screwed. And not in a good way. No recourse. No way out.

Except to get free. Right now.

Rhia jerked her hand loose. A fist connected with the side of Bryan's head, sending it sideways with a wicked snap. The jeweled dagger always strapped to her thigh was almost in her hand when the bastard dropped his full weight down on top of her. She just couldn't get a full breath. Her head spun. Wriggling black spots swam around her field of vision.

Ugh, she was going to throw up.

A backhand to the jaw didn't help. She hadn't seen the blow coming and now both her hands were above her head, held securely in his grip. His free hand brutally squeezed and twisted a tender breast. And he had an erection? Ewww.

She swallowed hard as more bile surged and her dinner bubbled threateningly at the base of her throat. Frustrated and angry, Rhia let out an ear-piercing scream when Bryan pushed his hand roughly underneath her tunic searching for the top of her leggings.

When the skin of a clammy hand touched the flesh of her belly, she went completely still.

"That's more like it, bitch," Bryan growled, yanking on her already ripped and torn clothing to expose her underwear. "I knew you would see things my way, Rhia. You always were a mewling little puke. It's your fault I ended up on the borders all those cycles. Your fault! If you hadn't run to your father blaming me for your making me angry, I would have surpassed your rank by now. You deserved a beating then, and you deserve one now."

Wasn't there an old proverb in the ancient books that said pride goes before destruction? Obviously the man wasn't much of a history reader.

In his haste to dip into her goodies, he released her hands to get a better grip on her bottoms. Her elbow crashed into the middle of his throat. Suddenly he was the one having trouble breathing.

Now wasn't that just too bad?

Knee to the groin preceded a full-contact left hook. He rolled completely away, eyes watering as he gasped through his bruised windpipe. It seemed he couldn't decide whether to hold his throat and gag, hold his balls and moan, or soothe his swelling eye.

On her feet, she yanked up her leggings and retrieved her blade from the carpet near the door. The corner of her mouth lifted at the exact moment Bryan realized the only way out was through her securely locked balcony windows or the front door. The first option was a no go. But a four story fall wasn't high enough to knock any sense into his hard head anyway. And unfortunately, Rhia and her blade stood in front of option number two.

There was a third option—part him from the family jewels he'd tried to force on her moments ago.

"You wouldn't kill a man in cold blood. You don't have it in you." But the quaver in his voice said he didn't believe his own words. He knew she'd do it. Knew she'd shred him. Sweat dripped from his brow and trailed down his clammy pale skin like wax down a spent candle.

Neither of them heard the door open.

Chapter Three

His party had shown none of their discomfort or concern in their expressions at the suddenly pressing journey back to Draema Proper. In fact, if not for the chilling mounds of snow piled along the roads and the biting winds, it would have been a good time under clear, and amazingly vivid, blue skies.

They'd moved quickly through the buffer zone that separated Draema Seine from the capital of the province, Draema Proper. In the distance, the High City had been a welcome sight, rising from the heart of these lands. Built in the middle of its seven colonies, this was the most advanced area in the world. The dawning sunlight had reflected various shades of pink and purple off both the inner, and outer walls; all of which were built with the famous, silvery-white Draeman stone.

Sleek buildings were shaded by tree-lined walks, which led into vast, city squares. The High City boasted a mix of rolling hills, and neatly-groomed pastures alongside well-kept roads. Some were laid with cobblestone, while others were covered by a smooth, dark, magnetized substance that allowed the passage of small conveyances called 'hovers'. Horses were still used here for sport, but inner-to-outer city travel typically meant a ride in one of the neat little vehicles, or a spot on the train. RuArk preferred the wild, open spaces of his own province, but didn't hesitate to admit this place held wonder for those who appreciated such things.

He'd brought more than thirty men on this journey, but only RuArk and a single fireteam of six warriors had passed through the open City gates this morning. There were very few of his people in this place, yet he'd been immediately recognized. The advantage of being son of the ruler of the neighboring province was being waved through the towering gates quickly. Well, that, and the reputation of being a ruthless bastard that took down enemies hard and fast with no promise to ask questions later.

Through a second set of lower walls that surrounded the Citadel, the High Council's right-hand, Mannon, had greeted them and rushed them into a meeting. From this morning's arrival, until leaving the High Counsel's chambers moments ago, they'd worked through one planning session after another until everything was in place.

Though so tired his muscles weighed down his bones as he dragged himself toward the guest apartments, RuArk could not ignore the flash and tensing of excitement that tapped at his gut. As if something long dead was waking inside him, stretching and unfurling itself in anticipation of seeing where this new turn in life would lead.

And Rhia was smack in the middle of this, this...whatever it was.

And in spite of the intrigue surrounding the danger to the woman, what would occur between them would be hot as the mid-Summer sun. He'd known from the *Seeking*, had felt it as he'd replayed that vision over and over in his mind. Damn near ached for it now that he knew the woman was somewhere near. Strange, he still hadn't seen the flesh and blood star of his *Seeking* vision. But he would soon enough.

RuArk steered his First Commander, Sharyn, toward a wide archway that opened into a large, starlit atrium. The space was filled with lush green trees, shrubs and a little stone bench where one could sit and enjoy the sun or moon overhead. At the rear of the atrium, two sets of mirroring staircases took off up the tower walls to a landing; where tall arches led opened to wide hallways. The stairs continued up the walls, winding their way upward to another landing, and yet another.

Finally they were at the top. There were no hallways or arches—only two doors separated by a ten-meter wide, colorful mural of the Draeman countryside.

He'd just pressed the key against the wall lock of the rooms he would share with Sharyn when a panic-inducing yell rang through the tower. He looked toward the sound and cursed.

Sharyn's gasp of surprise, followed by her quiet chuckle made him grimace. He hadn't meant to say that out loud, especially in the presence of a lady. The High Counsel put him in this part of the Citadel to keep an eye on Rhia. He'd hoped the job could wait until she returned from the made-up errand they'd created for her at Harbor Station.

"Apparently not," RuArk muttered and moved quickly towards the source of the noise. Through her slightly open door, two voices were clearly heard, both of them yelling. Not wanting to be mistaken for an intruder, he opened the door carefully, just enough to peek inside. The scene that met him was…wrong. On too many levels to list.

A greasy looking fellow had Rhia flat on her back on the thick carpets, trying to rip her trousers off. She was obviously not cooperating. The man's fist connected with her jaw. The blow should have knocked her out, but Rhia was moving and moving quickly. Her next breath saw her up off the floor and brandishing a wicked, long blade. A katana made in the old style.

Her intent was clear — skin the greaser.

Rhia's hair was dark, fire streaked and tangled all over her head. But the blood. There was so much blood. It was on her face, streaming down her neck from her eyes, nose and mouth to soak the collar of her top.

RuArk kept his expression neutral, but he really wanted nothing more than to rip the greaser in half. Hell, he might not love Rhia yet, but it was only a matter of time considering the Ancestors clearly meant for him to have her. The moment he'd accepted the *Seeking* she'd been given into his care. And this man dared to threaten her? Not bloody likely.

His first thought was to kick the door in the rest of the way, stride across the room and grab the idiot by his scrawny neck. But he'd be a fool to simply stroll into the room and surprise a woman with a sharp blade in her hands and hellfire in her eyes.

In spite of the obvious injuries, her fighting form was perfect; her handling of the blade smooth and experienced. She held no fear and knew she was in position to deliver a killing blow. And he couldn't blame her one bit. In truth, it was Rhia's ability to handle her visitor that helped keep RuArk's anger in check.

RuArk anticipated her move, knew the exact moment she'd decided to slice open the greaser's chest. What was she thinking? The scandal it would cause — a man in her rooms this time of night, and a dead man at that. Not to mention all the blood and guts that would have to be cleaned up.

And it would ruin his investigation.

One step through the door, RuArk called out.

"Excuse me. Is there a problem here?"

* * * * *

Rhia glanced away from the groveling swine on the floor and looked into a pair of eyes of such a wondrous mix of gray and silver, they reminded her of the waters off of Draema's southern coast.

RuArk Miwatani—the bane of her childhood existence. A bane she hadn't seen in so long she was surprised she recognized him. It was the eyes. Stormy sea, silver-as-fog, captivating eyes. Simply unforgettable. Ever. She had to look up a bit to meet his gaze, but once she caught it, Rhia was stuck right there.

Blazes, he was simply breath-stopping. Gone were the boyish good looks and mischievous expression. In their place was an angular jaw, high cheekbones and the confidence of a man.

A long, thick, black-as-sin braid was pulled forward over his shoulder to brush against the middle of his stomach. His skin, though quite a bit fairer than her own, was such a warm bronze that even now, at the end of mid-winter, he appeared to have spent a good deal of time under the glorious sunshine. He wore an unadorned, dark gray, fine gauged tunic, with dyed-to-match trousers. The outline of thick, roped muscle was visible beneath the supple material.

He closed in on her with a step so light she still didn't hear his footballs even though she was looking right at him.

And how the hell was she noticing this in the middle of a life or death struggle?

And what the hell was he doing here?

As far as she was concerned he was yet another man in her space without her damn permission. Enough gawking. Back to business.

Rhia returned her attention to the weasel groaning on the floor and raised her katana for the final blow. But before she could take a step, RuArk grabbed Bryan by the collar of his finely appointed cloak, and the back of his finely appointed trousers, hauled him out the door, and tossed him down the closest staircase.

While Bryan tumbled, Rhia's attention remained on RuArk. Sure, his expression was firm but she could tell he was totally enjoying this.

She looked him dead in the eye—or tried to, given his typical tree-like Gaian height—and proceeded to tear his head off with her tongue.

"Look, asshole. I know you warrior types are used to throwing the muscle around, but this is Draema. Here, people don't interfere unless they're asked to interfere. If I'd needed help I would have…"

Mouth snapped shut. The most beautiful

woman she'd ever seen stood directly behind the most ruggedly handsome man she'd ever known. Humph.

Bone straight, thick, and black-as-midnight hair was partially covered with a length of translucent silk that could only be described as sensual. Actually, her entire outfit seemed to be one big wispy scarf. Her skin reminded Rhia of the summer fruits that, according to the histories, used to grow in the now non-existent southern locales so long ago.

"Peaches," Rhia whispered, though she truly hadn't meant to.

And if this female had stood here the whole time, then she'd seen Rhia act a complete fool.

"Blasted hell," she muttered.

Rhia knew her hair was a tangled mess. Her face was swelling and surely beginning to display various colors in addition to sweat and blood. She wasn't sure why she cared that this man might compare her raggedy, torn appearance to this exotic woman. Nope, she shouldn't give a bloody goddamn...but she did. In fact, she flew past 'caring' and skidded to a halt at 'mortified'.

She scowled. Maybe the blows Bryan had landed on her face had shaken her brain loose because there was no way she should notice how ridiculously delicious RuArk's lips looked with that bit of a smile spread over them. Gah.

"What do you want? Aren't you far from home?" she snapped, forcing a blizzard into her words.

"You screamed. Loudly," he said quietly as he stepped toward her slowly, carefully. His words may have been just as frosty as hers, but the look he gave was equal parts 'smoking hot' and 'royally pissed'. "I can't resist taking care of such a beautiful lady, especially if she's in distress."

RuArk's voice slid over Rhia's frazzled nerves like warm, honey syrup while his expression took on a mysterious quality; like he could see through her funky-assed mood straight into her head, to uncover all the secret thoughts swirling around in there. Thoughts of him.

"Anything else I can do to assist you?" he asked quietly, though no less firm and as bossy as ever. And he was entirely too close now and looking at her as if he knew something she didn't. Her ice began to melt. Fast. She shivered, but not from fear nor an adrenaline crash.

It was anticipation? But of what? And who?

Not RuArk, for sure.

After all, she'd known this man forever. Though he'd been a boneheaded, spoiled, king's son, she'd carried a torch for this particular pain-in-the-ass for years. Memories she'd pushed to the very fringe of her mind peeked its head up and over the ragged edge of her conscience.

She remembered RuArk, putting straw in her hair. RuArk besting her at wooden blade practice. RuArk pulling stupid pranks on her, and getting her in trouble with both their fathers.

Sigh.

RuArk holding her hand at her mother's funeral, wiping the tears from her cheeks and telling her it would be okay. RuArk wrapping her in his cloak while she huddled in misery as they left the burial grounds so far away in Gaia province.

RuArk singing to her—quite badly at the top of his lungs—on her tenth birthday after talking his father into bringing him on an unscheduled visit, just to give her a birthday present he'd made with his own hands.

RuArk telling her he was going away to train for his role as Protector of the Realm of Gaia.

RuArk, staying away for years.

But it didn't matter now. Since then, Rhia had made a couple of trips to her own personal hell and back. She'd become her own woman — a woman who would never need saving by anyone. Ever.

And that included the gorgeous man towering over her.

"You should visit the Physicians, Rhia. It's getting late. I will escort you, if you wish."

So he was trying to save her, and tell her what to do? Not. Her out-of-whack-ness dissolved, replaced by a wash of hot anger. And a bit of unexplainable fear. Rather than dealing with the latter, she squashed her emotions into the toes of her blood-spattered boots and straightened her already-ramrod spine.

"Fuck. Off. RuArk."

She nudged him out the door with the tip of her katana, and practically punched a hole in the wall lock panel. The door slammed shut. So what if her behavior was irrational. Who cared? Besides, nobody asked the big guy to appear out of nowhere? To toss that pig, Bryan, down the stairs when she would have rather given him a few choice cuts?

Did it matter she'd been a shrew to a man

who'd always set her pulse racing and put her senses on edge? Or that she'd bled all over the place in front of an exotic looking woman in a daringly sexy outfit, all after learning via a stupid note that she'd been stripped of everything that made her who she was?

Rhia stomped around her apartments hurling every curse word she'd ever heard her soldiers use, then switched over to a couple of different languages just to draw it out a bit longer. She soon found that growling and cursing weren't enough. She yelled her frustration to the top of her lungs.

* * * * *

"She was so grateful for your help. Really, I could tell just as she slammed the door in your face."

RuArk turned to scold a not-so-amused Sharyn, but snapped his mouth shut at Rhia's cursing, loud enough to hear through the thick door. Sharyn scowled but didn't say another word, choosing instead to disappear into their suite across the landing and head to her own bedroom.

As for RuArk, it had been a long time since

he'd had a reason to see humor in anything but a good fight, yet here he was smiling, then laughing outright. The sound rumbled up through his chest in a deep, full timbre. And all because of the fate the Ancestors handed him, a fate named Rhia.

Door secured, he slipped his blades underneath his pillow and burrowed down into the thick, downy bedding. Keen senses detected no danger as he relaxed and closed his eyes to meditate.

The rest of his men had slipped quietly into the City and settled into the non-descript, seldom used quest quarters on the far side of town. At dawn, Rhia would depart for Harbor Station on the errand they'd made up for her, and RuArk would visit the High Counsel to finalize the details of their plans.

After her behavior tonight, he almost wished the High Counsel was going to be the one breaking the news to the hellcat next door. Almost.

He and Rhia's first meeting after so many seasons had been far from expected. He'd expected happiness, and light, and fun...then again, he had enjoyed tossing the greasy fellow down the steps. In the end, it didn't matter whether Rhia liked that he was here for her or not, he had a job to do—keep her safe and make her his.

As he drifted off, the *Seeking* quest he'd taken after his visit from the Grandfather flashed to the forefront of his mind...

Carried on the arms of the Wind, RuArk looked down upon the land with admiration. The beautiful, rolling hills were covered by a spectacular white, snowy blanket that sparkled like diamonds and luminescent pearls. The bright, full moon reflected off the frozen meadows. And there were so many stars. They filled the pre-dawn sky, twinkling their greeting to the Wind as It passed, carrying its companion.

Off in the distance RuArk spotted a faint glimmer on the ground. The light appeared to be a small campfire, out in the middle of the ice-covered lands. What would anyone be doing way out here in mid-winter? They circled around as RuArk searched for any signs of life. The place was deserted.

"What's going on here?" RuArk asked on a whisper.

The Wind gave no answer, but instead settled directly over the small flames, whipping them up into a firestorm. It flared wildly in spite of the snow covering the ground. The energy from the fire joined itself to that of the Wind, and the Wind became a great storm also. Side by side, the firestorm and the

windstorm grew together, reaching up into the starlit
sky until it seemed brightened by a second sun.

Then RuArk felt it, just as the Grandfather said.
A taint. A subtle hint of foul aura just out of reach,
focused on the flame. It faltered until it ceased to give
as much energy to its union with the Wind. As the
flame wavered, the windstorm and the firestorm were
both diminished. The mighty forces of nature became
nothing more than a slight breeze and a small
campfire once more.

Here, just as in the Dream, he didn't experience
true physical sensation, but only a fool would ignore
the trickle of apprehension slipping up his arms. He
turned to the North, but saw nothing. South, East
and West, all was silent. But he knew something,
someone, was out there. Perhaps multiple some ones.

After endless moments, he spotted a woman
alone in the night, gliding along the snow-covered
meadows. The sleek outline of her body was shrouded
in shadow. She moved with easy grace. Careful yet
confident, she possessed an inner strength that made
her appear more hunter than prey. Who was this
woman, now almost as near as his own skin?

Looking more closely, RuArk almost tumbled out
of the Seeking and back into his physical body in
surprise. The glow from her amber eyes pierced his
soul – Rhia Greysomne, daughter of the High
Counsel of Draema Province.

Oh, he remembered Rhia, stubborn and headstrong as a young girl. He was now being set on the path back to her as a woman. There was danger, yes, but he sensed that she needed something more than protection. But what could she need more than her own life?

It had been endless seasons since he'd seen her, yet even after all this time, and in this place, his body reacted strongly to her presence. Gods, her essence was exquisite; her aura strong and clean. She was not the source of the foulness on the air. But whoever, or whatever it was, seemed to follow her, long for her, covet her from a distance. Strange.

RuArk reached out but she didn't respond. Didn't seem to sense him at all.

Flashes of himself and Rhia in a loving embrace danced before his eyes. They smiled, touched, arms twined around each other as he loved her fiercely. Then there were stolen moments, a few quiet words shared.

My gods, she was his? A woman he'd thought of often, but hadn't pursued? Had longed for, but believed was out of reach? RuArk had no idea how things would develop, but it wasn't his to worry about. All he needed to do was find and stay on the path that had obviously been chosen for him. A path that led to Rhia Greysomne.

After accepting what had been shown to him that

night, he'd been returned to his physical body. And there he'd sat until gooseflesh had risen on his bare arms and legs. In fact, he'd watched the sunrise through the opening of the Seeking place and breathed in the lingering scent of sweet, warm female until it had completely faded away.

And now, the woman of his *Seeking* was just across the landing. Just out of reach. RuArk rolled over in his bed and let the memory of the *Seeking* continue to wash over him and fill his mind even as sleep claimed him. She was his, and he would protect her from whatever danger lurked here in Draema.

And RuArk couldn't wait to begin his new job.

About the Author

TJ is a USA Today and New York Times bestselling author, as well as an award-winner in several romance genres, including paranormal, fantasy, sci-fi and urban fantasy romance. A true Taurus, TJ isn't slowing down and she's definitely too stubborn to stop when she sees the fence!

No matter the genre TJ is penning, her favorite thing to do is build worlds. To take you somewhere extraordinary. To transport you to a place where you can close your eyes and slip into your fantasy…

Visit T.J. Michaels online at her website
www.TJMichaels.com

Also by Author TJ Michaels

Carinian's Seeker, Vampire Council of Ethics Book
One
Serati's Flame, Vampire Council of Ethics Book Two
Hatsept Heat, Vampire Council of Ethics Book Three
Seeker's Solace, Vampire Council of Ethics Book Four
Silk Road, Seals of Destiny
Spirit of the Pride, A Pryde Ranch Shifter Story
Niah's Pride, A Pryde Ranch Shifter Story
Pursuit of Pride and Pleasure, A Pryde Ranch Shifter
Story
Juicy, A Twilight Teahouse Story
Luscious, A Twilight Teahouse Story
Jaguar's Rule
Forever December
Egyptian Voyage
On the Prowl
Entwined Hearts
Elemental Heat
Caramel Kisses